CHTHONIC MATTER

A DARK FICTION QUARTERLY

Edited by

C. M. Muller

Winter 2024 (Volume 2, Issue 4)

© MMXXIV by Contributors

CONTENTS

Sticky
M. Stern
1

Basement Friend
Lene MacLeod
27

A Folded Letter
Neil Williamson
45

Dr. Fuller's Last Lecture
Logan McConnell
65

Wild Places
Tim Jeffreys
79

Mixed Signals
Michael McKeown Bondhus
103

Corpse Medicine
Kathryn Reilly
119

Undone
Warren Benedetto
129

STICKY

M. Stern

Everything was getting sticky. Will Sharpe first noticed it while touching the counter next to his stove. There was a sticky coating that he attributed to some combination of cooking splatters and the ungodly heat and humidity, which his air conditioner was barely denting. Curious as to how far the stickiness extended, he pressed his finger harder on the metal of the stove then pulled it away.

"*Gngh!*" he shouted. "*Dammit!*"

The coating was much stickier on the stove. He looked at his finger and saw that a layer of skin was torn from his fingertip. The skin flake stuck to the stove. Blood welled up around the shiny pink wound. He grabbed a Band-Aid from the cupboard and a bottle of all-purpose cleaner to attack the stove with. Just as he got the Band-Aid on, someone knocked.

It was late. This was unusual. He walked over and looked through the peephole. He saw his neighbor Colleen, drenched in sweat. He opened the door.

"Hey, you all right?"

"Power's out," she said. "Every unit but yours."

"You're kidding," Will said. He stood awkwardly for a moment, then said: "Oh, come in! Want some water? Here, sit."

He situated her on the living room futon, away from the kitchen and its mysterious stickiness. He went to the kitchen and returned with a glass of water.

"Call the landlord yet?" he asked, setting the glass down.

"Yeah, left a message," she said. "Brendan's in Phoenix. I had him call too. No luck. I've just been knocking on doors. Everyone else who lives here has somewhere to crash."

Brendan, Will gathered, was Colleen's boyfriend. The two lived in the apartment below him. The young couple had been there for years—a rarity, as people moved in and out of the big building quite frequently. Colleen showing up now was the most interaction he had experienced with them or any neighbor.

"You're welcome to the futon," Will said. "It's not super comfortable but—wish I had some beers."

"I brought this if you want," Colleen said.

Will was somewhat startled at the size of the bag of pot she pulled from her purse. He tapped his forehead earnestly and gave a thumbs up.

She placed a small blue pipe on the coffee table and began packing the bowl meticulously. Will searched under the futon and pulled out a lighter he remembered dropping there.

When he emerged, she handed him the pipe.

"Thanks kindly, neighbor," he said. He hit the pipe, taking polite care to blacken only one side of the contents, held the hit, handed the pipe back, and released a plume of smoke that terminated in an eye-reddening cough.

Colleen gestured at the water.

"Good," he croaked, reaching for it. "Real good one."

A few more passes back and forth and they were sitting in a silence that felt imposingly empty.

"Ever been in love?" Colleen said, shattering it.

"Uhm—I—"

"Weird question," she said. "I get it. I'm just curious. I'm in a loveless relationship. I've been with Brendan for ten years. We're more like roommates than a couple. Our interests have completely diverged. I sometimes feel like the only thing keeping us together is fear. Fear of change. Fear of how breaking up would look to our friends. Fear of telling our parents."

Will suddenly felt aware of how much he was blinking and wondered if it looked abnormal. He took a sip of water.

"So?" she said. "You? Share."

"*Love?*" Will said. "There's a person I write letters to, but I don't send them. I write poorly-written poems for her, but she'll never read them. Is that love? It's been seven years, I think. Her name is Mildred. I met her at a party. We were dating for six months. At least I think we were dating. It felt like a relationship. But I was afraid if I asked how seriously she was taking it, she would tell me I had the wrong idea. That she was seeing other people, or something. Looking back, near the end, I started unconsciously pushing her away. Being caustic, obnoxious, doing subtly hurtful things. Like I was punishing her. Daring her to hurt me back. Demanding she confirm my suspicion that she couldn't possibly care about me."

They both jumped at the sound of the air conditioner kicking back on. He continued.

"The relationship, whatever it was, petered out. It didn't bother me. I dated around. We would still text on and off. Then that ended, too. About a year later something in my head flipped. I don't really know why. I started thinking about her constantly. But I was terrified of trying to find her again. I wouldn't survive the humiliation if I called her and she was just indifferent, or on to something else, wondering why I would be calling her. You know? So I'm just waiting. Writing letters. Writing poems. It feels like it's taken on a mystical character. Removed from any reality of what she could *possibly* be. What is that? Love? Infatuation? I sometimes think I'm addicted to the romantic element of it all."

Will suddenly felt like the silence was staring at him, and he was horrendously nervous. It seemed possible he heard Colleen's question wrong. "You asked, right?" he said. "Love was the topic? I might be confused—"

"No, it's okay!" she said, scooting toward him. "It's a weird question. I didn't mean to freak you out. Uhm . . . Do you need me to—"

Oh God, he thought. I've done it. She's going to say *leave*.

He tried to read her expression but it seemed a series of still frames, each unintelligible. He knew he would feel better in a few hours. But now his faculties were compromised, tangled, lacking an anchor of objectivity. He was frozen with embarrassment. He started to apologize, just as she completed her thought.

"—suck your dick?"

Wasn't expecting that, Will thought. And such poetic phrasing. What's a need, what's a want? Then things were out and events unfolding, then culminating.

"C— C— Th— Th— *Shshsh*—" he said.

There was only silence and the quiet hum of the air conditioner that blended with it. Will felt like he and Colleen were silence's afterthoughts. Colleen had her face on his stomach where his shirt was pulled up, and idly traced circles with one finger below it. He was running his hand through her hair for some time. Then said:

"Sometimes I think my insides must be a mistake. I should be filled with light. Not a confusing mass of guts, shit, and borborygmi. I unscrewed a laptop yesterday. The apparent disorder inside was shocking. Stuff's shoved where it fits. It's a mess. No apparent connection with what happens on the screen. I thought it must be the same for surgeons. Seeing organs stuffed in bodies. I don't believe that disorder can be me. I don't see what my organs have to do with me."

"Do you always talk so much after?" she said without looking up.

"Only when I'm awake," he whispered, then fell asleep.

WILL SNORTED AWAKE in a sunbeam. He was still sitting, drool pouring down his chin. He hiked his shirt down and stood, sweating but feeling good. Past, perhaps, the years of life in which such excitement tends to occur, and all the more appreciative for it. Colleen must have left. Electricity must be fixed. He took the glass of water to the kitchen.

He placed the glass down on the counter and was startled when he looked at the stove. He scrutinized the Band-Aid on his finger, then looked back. The chunk of skin that had stuck there the previous night was gone.

Will leaned in, resting his forearm in front of the kitchen sink to get a better look. There was a mark where the skin had stuck on the stove. Something had taken it.

"Huh," he said, then: "*Yeow! Godfuh—*"

He grabbed his forearm, peeked under his hand and saw a portion of skin the size of a stick of gum torn cleanly away.

The counter in front of the sink was sticky.

He ran to the bathroom, got a bigger Band-Aid and some tweezers, bandaged the wound, crouched down and began picking at the skin he lost with the tweezers, trying to dislodge it from the counter.

The skin patch resisted the tweezers, adhering to the strange sticky substance with an unnatural affinity. Will scraped with frustration at the counter tile, carving lines with a chalkboard screech. It failed to loosen the affixed skin.

Will dropped the tweezers, grabbed his phone, walked to the living room, and dialed the landlord. He left a message:

"Hi, this is your tenant Will Sharpe. There's something sticky in my kitchen. I'm having trouble cleaning it off. I think it could be toxic.

Could you maybe send someone to look at it? Thanks!"

A FEW MORNINGS later Will went for a jog. He came back to his apartment, showered, walked out of the bathroom in a towel, and decided to grab a snack from the fridge. He took a few steps into the kitchen and grunted with surprise.

He looked down. His heel was stuck to the floor. He had stepped in a fluorescent green puddle that looked like gelled antifreeze.

He froze, gritted his teeth, and pulled his foot up.

He howled.

A silver dollar-sized chunk of skin tore from his heel with an agonizing dry sting, like at the edge of a torn callous. He stumbled back, dropped the towel and retched from the pain. Hopping to the bathroom, he ran his foot under ice-cold water. After an hour, his heel was merely throbbing. He bandaged it, hopped to his bedroom, and took a nap.

He awoke to a soft knocking at his door and felt a thrill. He threw his clothes on, including socks, and answered.

"Howdy neighbor," Colleen said, walking in. "I thought I left that there!"

She pointed to the paraphernalia still sitting on the table. As she collected it, she said:

"Got a funny question, do you have any duct tape I could borrow? Can't get it *anywhere* for some reason. I tried online and they canceled my order!"

Will nodded, ran to the kitchen, collected the tape, and put it on the table. Then said:

"Here's one for you. Have you noticed anything in your

apartment getting sticky?"

"Sticky?" she said. "In what way?"

"Some surfaces have a weird residue on them. It seems to be spreading. I'm wondering if it's—uh, bug excretion, or something. I've been calling the landlord every day but he's not answering. You haven't noticed anything?"

"Nope. Nothing," she said. "Good thing, too—we're doing an engagement party when Brendan gets back."

"Uh—engagement?" Will said, failing to mask the surprise in his voice.

She eyed him.

"Yes," she said. "We figured it was time to finally just go ahead and do it."

"Uhm, I think—we—"

Will could feel his face reddening.

"The thing the other night," she said, earnestly. "I hope you didn't read into that."

For the past few days, the thought of Colleen had been ramping up in Will's mind; of the incident itself and her in general. Unemployment gave him a lot of time to think—usually about Mildred. Colleen appearing bumped Mildred out of his mind almost immediately. It made him appreciate the time he had been wasting, consigning himself to a prison of pining. It seemed so silly, so juvenile, the second someone showed up bringing a new perspective.

The previous afternoon, with that new perspective in mind, he did something a long time coming.

He pulled his stack of letters and poems—*Mildred, oh Mildred, when I'm with you I'm so thrilled-ed,* and so on—from his desk drawer, and went to work on them with scissors. Half an hour later, a mound of confetti colored with indistinguishable fragments of his handwriting sat on his bed.

On a lark, feeling free, finally on to the next thing, whatever it may be, he began throwing fistfuls of the paper in the air.

His mood dimmed when he realized the paper was sticking to his bedroom walls.

His bedroom was getting sticky.

He wondered now if he should have taken that as an omen not to celebrate too hard.

"You showed up randomly at my apartment, talking about being stuck in a loveless relationship," Will said. "How should I have *read* that?"

Colleen sighed heavily.

"Stuck?" she said. "You know sometimes—you're inebriated—and your mind goes down a path that's true, but it's not the *only* truth? Like, two things can be true at once."

"So . . ."

"I wouldn't say I'm *stuck,*" Colleen said. "I wouldn't say it's *loveless*. I've had concerns. That's why Brendan and I have been experimenting with opening up our relationship."

Will felt a sinking feeling.

"You're swingers," he said.

"That's a little much," she said.

"But if I were looking for porn pertaining to your lifestyle, I would put 'swinger' in the search box."

"Look," she said. "You have a right to your feelings, but you don't need to be insulting. Yes, I could have clarified things better. But you must admit there was a cinematic quality to the moment. Those are the types of moments in life that I feel we should embrace. That I am *trying* to embrace. Can't it just be that?"

"I guess?" Will said. "I just don't really want to get in the middle of anyone's . . . arrangement. And I don't think you're being fully honest with yourself ab—"

She smarted with a palpable heat at the evocation of honesty, and interrupted:

"Not honest with *my* self? Says the guy who's attracted to impossible situations. Admit it. You're hung up on some girl you haven't talked to in years. I bet if she showed up begging you to get married and move to the suburbs tomorrow, you'd lose interest immediately."

"You *barely* know me," Will said. Seeing what this was turning into, he said:

"Hey, let's calm down, take a step back, and pretend this never happened. I'm sorry I was insulting."

"I apologize for being insulting too," she said, earnestly. "And I agree. Time to move forward."

"Okay, cool," Will said.

"Should I leave?"

"Yeah, probably."

There was a long silence.

"Need me to suck your dick first?"

Ten minutes later they sat there on the futon, her head on his stomach.

"Sometimes I swear I can feel the Earth's rotation," he said. "I'll be laying on my bed and feel like the spinning Earth might throw me off. I feel like a thin-bodied bug or an insignificant dry flake of a leaf, vulnerable to the slightest gust. I don't understand what gravity has to do with me. I like how you weigh me down. I feel plausibly heavy now."

"We'll have to work on the talking," she whispered.

A MOMENT AFTER Colleen left, Will was certain something had scuttled across the floor. He walked into the kitchen and saw it darting into a crack.

He looked at the floor and groaned.

The skin from his heel was gone.

Struck with sudden inspiration, Will grabbed a toenail clipper and clipped a chunk of dead skin from his other foot. He took a mousetrap from a kitchen drawer, hot-glued the skin to the trap's catch, placed it on the counter next to the sink, and carefully set the trap.

Satisfied that he was moving toward managing the problem, he casually slid the Band-Aid down from his finger to survey his skinned fingertip.

He noticed a tiny white crystal at the center of the wound. He felt a chill, and quickly replaced the Band-Aid.

FOR A COUPLE mornings in a row Will ran out into the kitchen, dodging the sticky spots, looked at the trap and found, with both relief and disappointment, nothing. After a week, one night at around midnight, he was in bed and, just as he drifted off to sleep, thought he heard the trap snap in the kitchen.

The next morning he entered the kitchen and his heart fluttered. The trap was upside-down. Will reached to flip it over.

Woah! — He jumped back. Whatever was trapped rattled

briefly and frantically.

He grabbed a plastic broom. Holding it near the bristled end, he pointed the handle at the trap and slowly edged toward it like he was feeling out a fencing partner. He counted to three and knocked the trap off the counter.

It clattered to the floor and landed right-side up.

He dropped the broom, crouched, and assessed the trap.

The thing pinned beneath the metal bar of the mousetrap resembled a rectangular, jet-black block of Jell-O. It was compressed across its center by the bar, and had four small, white chitinous structures curved like overgrown dog toenails affixed to either side. The dry flake of Will's skin jutted halfway out of the thing's front. It had begun to absorb it.

Will grabbed the broom again, and fetched his dustpan. He positioned them around the trap to sweep it up.

He tripped back.

The thing shrieked.

The side that dangled off the trap was filling with air and deflating through two pea-sized anterior orifices. The spasmodic deflation created a wet, warbling, oddly human sound.

"Shut up!" Will shouted. "*Dammit!*"

Will tripped over a takeout box, grabbed it and threw it at the thing. Instead of quieting, it began trying to free itself. Its four nail structures spun rapidly. Will jumped over it and grabbed from the counter a bottle of all-purpose cleaner.

He aimed, growled, and sprayed repeatedly, showering the gelatinous block with squirts of cleaner.

The thing struggled more intensely. Its scream became a gurgle. Two meat-pink structures lined with mucus prolapsed from its sound orifices. The thick scent of wet, rotting meat floated up from it. Will gagged. He pulled his shirt over his nose, threw open a cabinet and grabbed one bottle of hydrogen peroxide and one of rubbing alcohol.

He emptied out both onto the struggling thing.

At the first splashes the thing's black surface developed a soupy oil-slick sheen. The pink extensions strained further out until they resembled tongues, flapped chaotically, and desiccated to jerky. The thing hissed dryly, becoming disfigured and swelling. The nails blackened. The tongue-side end split and an irritated red organ hemorrhaged out. The surface bubbled into black pustules, which swelled into tentacles of ash like black snake fireworks.

The whole thing was soon a crumbled ashen pile.

Will sucked his lip. He called his landlord and left a message.

Whatever these things were, he needed to keep them out. He assessed the apartment and saw numerous cracks where they could be sneaking in. He went to grab some duct tape from the drawer.

Dammit, he thought.

BRENDAN STOOD IN the doorway of the apartment in a sleeveless shirt. Will felt like Brendan was staring into his soul.

"Hey! You're upstairs, right? Is it Bill? Come in! Want a beer?"

"Will," Will said, following the guy and taking the beer. "I'm just dropping by to get the tape Colleen, uh, borrowed."

"Oh right! She mentioned she bumped into you."

Will searched for tension in the way Brendan said that, but

heard none, and followed the guy. After ten minutes or so of boring conversation, Will asked:

"Have you noticed anything in your apartment getting sticky?"

"Nope, Col' makes sure we keep it pretty tidy around here. She's got me well-trained on cleaning spills, know what I'm sayin'?"

Will nodded politely at the comment as Brendan handed him the duct tape. Will glanced at the bathroom, and something struck him suddenly as odd.

"You've got in-unit laundry in your bathroom?" Will said. "In this building?"

"Oh yeah," Brendan said. "Wore the landlord down on that one. You know this building is so old we've got a laundry chute in there? This weird little door."

"Is that what that is," Will said. "Uh—speaking of bathrooms—"

Will raised the empty beer.

"All yours," Brendan said.

In the bathroom there was a pile of bed sheets in front of the washing machine. Will went first to the wall, pushed the small door open, and saw that the chute went upwards, connecting presumably to the analogous door in his apartment.

He ran the water and sat, thinking. Staring at the pile of sheets, he noticed movement.

Slowly he reached down.

He moved the sheet on the top.

A gelatinous black rectangle scurried away. Will stifled a scream.

He washed his hands and face in the sink, gave a performative flush, and went back out.

He was about to dig further into the matter with Brendan, but thought better of it.

"Hey we're having a party on the tenth next month, if you're interested," Brendan said as Will was on the way out.

"Maybe!" he replied politely.

Back in his apartment, Will was furiously duct-taping closed the old laundry chute and numerous other parts of the apartment. As he did, questions weighed heavily on his mind:

Why was his apartment getting sticky and not his neighbor's?
Why were those things crawling around in his neighbor's laundry?
Why did it all start when Colleen paid him a visit?

He had a hard time getting to sleep that night in the horrendously humid room, wrestling through those questions and trying to piece together if—and how—he was these people's target.

WILL WOKE UP, jaw clenched tight and muscles aching from a heavy, anxious sleep. He noticed something was wrong before his eyes opened. He sat bolt upright.

"No," he said. "*No!*"

He scrambled to the bathroom. The mirror confirmed his tongue's discovery. His canine teeth were gone. He began brushing his remaining teeth furiously and through tears, as if such vigor would bring the missing ones back. He swished and spit and threw down the toothbrush and sobbed.

He stumbled out into his living room, picked up his phone, dialed his dentist, and received a busy signal.

He threw himself down on the couch.

All of these things were connected. He just had to figure out how. He needed a clearer view of what was happening.

He had an idea.

THE NEXT MORNING, the blistering sun took on a purple tint beaming through the window. The windows were getting sticky. Will awoke bathed in sweat, yet something in him celebrated.

He was missing another tooth.

Dashing to his living room, he fumbled with his smartphone. He opened the app for the motion-triggered surveillance camera he had set up the previous afternoon, and found the captured video from the previous evening.

He saw himself on-screen, sleeping. The footage switched between a shot of the full room and a close-up of his face.

Watching, he noticed something entering the frame. He sucked nervously at the new gap in his mouth.

A gelatinous rectangle crawled onto his bed, tottering like a cheap toy.

Knew it, he thought.

Will observed the thing make its way from the comforter onto his own sleeping face.

He whimpered at what came next.

The thing paused on his sleeping chin. From its anterior emerged a whip-like feeler. The feeler's end searched under Will's sleeping nose. It pulled back cautiously at a snore, then continued as his breathing normalized. Eventually it found his upper lip.

A needle extended from the tip of the feeler. It pierced the skin of his lip. The gelatinous rectangle shivered with peristaltic pumping.

The thing withdrew its needle and a second feeler emerged. This one snaked under Will's lip, now numbed, and gently lifted it up. The first feeler, with its needle, jabbed carefully into the upper portion of Will's revealed gums.

The needle pulled back again and retracted into its feeler. From that same feeler emerged a drill, slightly shorter than a quarter-inch.

The drill spun up with a piercing whine. Beneath where its twin feeler held up Will's lip, the spinning drill lowered itself to his top-left incisor. Its whine down-tuned as it drilled into the biting edge of the tooth.

The drill buried itself to the hilt and halted with a crunch.

The rectangle began ambling backwards until it was on the comforter and the feeler was pulled taught. It kept pulling, its nail structures moving in laborious rotations. It stumbled as the tooth was uprooted. Both feelers retracted. It pulled Will's pilfered incisor halfway into its anterior and was on its way.

Will closed the app, shut his eyes, and thought for a moment.

Nervously, he pulled the larger Band-Aid up from his forearm and quickly replaced it.

On the healing wound, there were unmistakable clusters of glassy white inorganic fibers.

"I'm going *insane!*" he growled. He smashed his phone on the floor.

He reached down to pick it up.

It stuck there.

He wept.

WILL WAS BARELY sleeping these days, and when he slept he inevitably woke up missing an additional tooth. His diet was almost entirely milkshakes now. There was a part of him that believed, on some level, that none of this would be happening if he had only stayed with Mildred, though he could not figure out how. In fact he could figure out very little. Colleen had not dropped by since he retrieved the duct tape, and he was thankful. The more his mind ground over the issue, the more it was obvious that she and her boyfriend had a hand in this—whatever *this* was.

Just as he had that thought, there was a pounding on the door. Will threw on his surgical mask and answered.

"We've gotta have a talk here, Bill," said Brendan, pushing his way into the apartment. Colleen was behind him.

"You people won't *get me*," snarled Will. "Whatever your plans! Whatever these—things—are—"

The couple argued past his protestations without acknowledgment.

"You're being irrational!" shouted Colleen at her boyfriend. "Stop this nonsense!"

Brendan sat on the futon, tapping the coffee table nervously. Finally he said:

"Colleen just told me that you have engaged in—"

He clenched his teeth for a moment, then finished:

"—*intimacy.*"

"You *told* him?" Will said, facing Colleen. "That's a real violation—"

"He *likes* it," she snarled back. "He likes it when I tell him but he doesn't *like* it that he likes it! That's why he's acting like a jealous baby right now!"

"I don't want anything to do with this damn shit!" Will pleaded. "Get out of my—"

Colleen positioned herself behind Will.

"He's got a *huge one*," she hissed at Brendan over Will's shoulder.

"*No!*" Will said. "I don't—Really? You'd say huge?"

Brendan snarled, stood up, and lunged.

"Woah!" said Will, tripping back. Colleen dodged out of the way. Brendan grabbed Will's T-shirt with both hands. Will loosened the grip as Brendan cocked his fist, stumbled, and slipped Brendan's punch. With his missed punch, Brendan's ring and pinky fingers grazed the wall.

"*Whu? Whu?*" Brendan said, suddenly sickly pale.

Colleen shrieked.

Brendan's two fingers remained affixed to the wall. The wall was sticky. He cradled the wounded hand in his other. Blood poured to the floor.

"What have you done to him!" she screamed, charging and grabbing Will's throat. She wrestled him toward his bookshelf. He said, in between bouts of slapping her hands away:

"Me!? This is *your* fault you psychos! Whatever you're doing to make things *sticky!* Whatever did—*this!*"

He pulled down his surgical mask.

His toothless mouth startled her. It gave him a second. He got behind her and put her in an arm-bar. Then he was tackled from behind.

He fell forward and so did Colleen. Her head struck the wall. There it stuck.

She jerked her head back. A large portion of her forehead, scalp, and hair remained on the wall.

"Oh my—*no!*" Will said. "Colleen! I— "

"I feel sorta funny," she mumbled, stumbling drunkenly toward Brendan.

Brendan howled and lunged at Will.

"I didn't *do this!*" Will said.

With Brendan's good hand, he pushed Will into the bookshelf. The full shelf tipped. Will dodged out of the way. The shelf collapsed on Brendan and Colleen as Will fell flat on his face on the floor.

Face pressed to the ground, he tried to push himself up.

Most of Will's cheek stuck to the ground and ripped off with the ease of separating wet tissue paper. He let out a cry from his mostly toothless maw, which now gaped open to the back gums on one side. Blood flooded down. He reached up with one hand and the full skin hand-print remained on the sticky floor.

Why, he thought. *Why me? Why any of this?* He collapsed back to the ground, howling and weeping and gurgling in his own pooling fluids. Each second a new wave of razor-sharp pain deserving of its own distinct name washed over him.

He saw the rectangles scuttling across the ground, coming for the neighbors. And for him.

And his last thoughts before losing consciousness were:
Gotta call the landlord—
Wouldn't have happened if—
Mildred—
Sticky—

HE WAS STILL there, after some indeterminate time. He was there, and the pain had stopped. *Why do some survive and others don't?* he thought. *Why are some selected?*

He was still there.

Everything was sticky.

There was no surface or object in the apartment that was not sticky. Will perceived the subtle differences in the sticky films with some new autonomic knowledge of the variations of stickiness. Gradations of stickiness revealed themselves to him with unimaginable nuance. On the kitchen floor alone, he saw 1,306 different types of sticky. Sticky was his only interest and his only friend. Will spent all day studying the stickiness of his footsteps and the physics of stickiness.

Will, whose flesh was now a metal impervious to stickiness. Will, whose skin was stripped by the residue and harvested by its gelatinous minions—and replaced. Weeks, months, or years ago. What remained human in Will's mind stood outside of time. Time was measured by biological processes no longer applicable.

Back when he first pulled himself up from the floor, his neighbors gone and presumably digested, he walked to the mirror and assessed himself—feeling like he was forgetting a lot but feeling all right. His face was a silver, skeletal mask, his mouth a grate with thin vertical slits, his eyes two ruby rectangles under his brow. His body was a silver analogue of his physique at peak fitness, with complex networks of trestles and pistons building points of articulation into each joint.

Now Will walked to the window. He pulled open the shade. The light it let in was a deep purple. He felt it calling him.

For the first time since his transformation, Will Sharpe went outside.

THE BLINDING PURPLE gleam of a blinding purple sun. A gleam carried on a heat that pulled water from bone and sound from scream. Even Will's impervious metal skin felt its heat. The purple glinted off his silver body vibrantly. In front of him, triangular puddles of sticky tessellated geometrically across former lawns. Sap-like stickiness wept from blackened trees. Clothes littered sidewalks and cars were embedded in houses— evidence of a failed mass exodus through which Will had slumbered, all sticky. Will took in the scene and looked at the sun and saw a thick black rectangle bisecting the blinding purple star like an octopus's retina.

It spoke into his mind, saying:

Go.

Will knew where to walk the way a lost cat knows its way home.

He entered the basement of his building, approached the boiler room, tore a grate off the wall, and crawled into the tunnel behind it.

After crawling on his belly for half a mile, the tunnel opened up so he could stand. The tunnel was sticky. Will noticed the city's pests decorating the tunnel walls in a state of arrest; many dead, some dying. Rats were frozen and twitching in any imaginable position, crowded like flies on flypaper. Bats hung from their feet, faces, and wings.

Eventually the tunnel terminated in a chamber.

There he saw The Others.

About fifty Others who had undergone this same arcane physiological replacement.

The room's floor was a metallic purple, patterned with complex fractals. Unlike the tunnel, though, there were no pests struggling in it. He soon realized this was because of the gelatinous things. Each time a beetle, mouse, or moth landed, a rectangle would appear, envelop the pest, and abscond.

Will's attention turned to the chamber's front. There hung two pendulous, flesh-like sacs the size of automobiles. They clung to the high chamber ceiling like they had been woven there by insects. He went nearer to them, and looked to his right.

Mildred.

The body was metal, the features indistinguishable from his own—but he knew it was her. Somehow, he knew.

He felt the invisible light within him brighten and shimmer. Brighter than the crying purple sun and its polygonal eclipse, so bright was his loving-delight at the presence of Mildred. He had no mouth to speak and no words that would do it justice in any case. He simply stood shoulder to shoulder with her, looking at her as she looked straight ahead. His mind flipped through memories and raced down pathways shut off since the transformation. He longed. Longed for some confirmation it was her. He felt like something inside him was screaming, howling for a reply. He stared, hoping for acknowledgment.

All heads suddenly turned to the sacs.

Will's hand swung and he believed he felt it graze hers.

Between the two sacs, there was a purple flash.

Will looked down at his chest.

A purple beam was directed at him.

He felt a tickling sensation. The beam was searing into him. It carved a plate from his chest, which fell out and clattered to the ground.

There they were.

Will's body cavity was empty save for being filled with the gelatinous things. Not just the black ones he knew. The creatures that filled him were a rainbow of different colors. Some solid, some striped, some translucent.

He thought:
This
This
This
Isn't
Isn't
Isn't
What
What
What
I—
I—
I—

Will was no longer seeing or thinking from a single discrete consciousness. He was diffusing into the beings that filled him.

The hundred-some Wills poured out with a series of wet plops and scattered, carried on impulse and instinct. His empty metal husk clanked to the ground, as the others around him did.

The will of each Will drove him to scuttle up the walls and ceiling and onto the sacs. There, all in the room communed, licking and scraping away the wrinkled, stinking layers of flesh that constituted them.

The sacs began to give way, and there was a celebratory pheromonal air exuded from the gelatinous community. They were thrown to the floor. Some hemorrhaged on impact, flopping and twisting like fish out of water, but all death and suffering was in the service of celebration.

A trickle of milk-white sticky where the sacs were punctured gave way to a flood as they tore fully open. In the midst of each flood dropped a thin, curled body.

From multiple vantage points, Will indulged in the splendor. The two gods sleepily uncurled their bodies and shimmied off the white, sticky fluid to reveal austere, thin humanoid forms with limbs like black gnarled wood. Each head was a featureless black rectangle set horizontally with three claw-like appendages on either end.

Before them, the gelatinous rectangles bathed in the sacred toxin, privileged to boil and rot for their gods. Will, Mildred, love, desire; wisps, ghosts, memories receding into unending black amnesia.

Surface. Substratum. Substance.
Sticky! Sticky! Sticky!

M. STERN is an author of weird horror, sword & sorcery, and science fiction whose stories have appeared in nearly two dozen magazines and anthologies, including *Weirdbook*, *From Beyond The Threshold*, and *Necronomi-RomCom*. If you're interested in reading about the latest sticky situations and horrific creations spilling out of his imagination, visit www.msternauthor.com.

BASEMENT FRIEND

Lene MacLeod

The subterranean landscape hadn't changed much. Standing on the bottom step of the spiral staircase, Fiona looked over the back section of the basement, which belonged to the upper flat. She had lived upstairs with her parents until she was old enough to flee.

She remembered the smell of wet laundry hanging on the clothes-lines spanning the basement. Her mother always brought Fiona down with her on laundry day. Fiona hadn't minded, the basement was filled with all kinds of old things to discover. Now it was her job to clear the space out and put the duplex up for sale. *It'll take weeks*, she thought, gazing over the stacks of boxes, trunks, and forgotten furniture. The old wringer washing machine was still there, even though her parents had a modern washer and dryer installed upstairs years ago. She did a cursory round, peeking into things and wiping away cobwebs. There was no way she was going to haul everything up those stairs. Instead, she'd walk through the front section of the divided basement to carry things outside.

She tried not to look, but she noticed anyway—the obvious contour line of the newer cement meeting the old where the hole in the floor was patched. She sensed fingers clawing at her—*just a memory*, and she ran upstairs, slamming the door. That "newer" cement had been placed many years ago.

FIVE-YEAR-OLD Fiona had been thinking about the dirt since the last laundry day. This time, she remembered to bring her pail and shovel downstairs. "I get to play in a sandbox, even during winter!" she said, scraping the plastic shovel through the gritty earth.

"Be careful with that dirt. Don't get it all over the basement," her mother said. No worries about toxins or insects or . . . anything. The cement had started to crack in the autumn, and when it became rubble Fiona's father had scooped up the broken pieces to throw away, saying he'd patch it when he had time.

As a winter baby it would be the next school year before Fiona could attend kindergarten, and this "sandbox" might help keep things fun.

SHE RESTED IN what had been her parents' bedroom. On the nightstand was the stack of flyers. Her mother had once mentioned she collected the junk mail and liked to look through it at bedtime, her version of light reading. Fiona's childhood bedroom, the room off the kitchen, had been converted into a laundry room and pantry, which was fine with Fiona—too many nightmares had been born there. Her father had passed years earlier, but her mother only two weeks ago—unexpectedly. A senior falling down steps was not an entirely rare event. Unlike the spiral basement staircase, the front stairs provided a straight tumble to the floor and to a broken neck.

Her knocking at the downstairs flat brought a middle-aged woman to the door.

"Hi, uh, Mrs. Kavas?"

"Yes . . . " The woman peered cautiously up at Fiona from behind the half-opened door.

"I'm Fiona. My mother was your landlady; and, well, I guess I am now!"

"We paid the rent. It comes out of the bank automatically—"

Fiona explained that she was not there to collect money but to let the tenant know she would be going back and forth through the front basement door. "I'll have a bin parked on the lawn for junk. If you have any little things to get rid of feel free to toss them in."

"No junk. Please don't come into my flat without asking."

"No, just the basement. It will take a couple of weeks at least."

Mrs. Kavas did not seem pleased in the least by this information. With a nod of her head, she closed the door, but not before the sound of laughing and running feet escaped. Fiona wanted to knock again to ask who all lived downstairs, then decided she would just look up the lease, which was in the packet of papers the lawyer had given her.

"I'M GETTING TIRED," little Fiona said, sitting in the dirt. They had been building roads and castles for almost an hour. Her friend was being so bossy. Fiona hated that. She hadn't expected that when she first heard the voice.

She had been playing in her "sandbox," while her mother did the laundry, mumbling to herself. *I wish I had someone to play with. Why can't I go to school?*

"I will play," a little girl's voice whispered, and Fiona jumped. "Don't be scared. I am coming soon. I will play with you. Do you like toys?"

"Yes, I do."

"Bring toys. I like toys, too."

With each trip to the basement, the girl in the dirt talked more, always whispering, always when the noisy washer was going. She told Fiona to bury a toy pony in the dirt, which she did and then she couldn't find it. The pony was gone.

That afternoon, while her mother watched soap operas, Fiona went to the basement. "Can I have my pony back now?"

The floor rumbled and she thought the pony would be pushed up through the dirt. Instead, she saw a hand. Thin fingers with long nails emerged from the dirt, followed by a second hand, two bony arms and finally a head and body.

Fiona jumped back, a gasp escaping her as chills crept up her spine.

"Don't be scared," the shadowy girl from the earth whispered. "I came to play, remember?"

Fiona felt weird, but she tried to have fun. A friend, right there in the basement with her was supposed to be fun. The girl had bright aqua eyes, the irises ringed with brilliant violet, and fair hair coated in wet soil and gritty sand. She wore only a sundress, also covered in dirt. Not just the dirt disguised this strange friend, but the basement lights cast dark shadows on her, especially the face. Fiona could never say for sure what the girl looked like.

"You are Fiona?"

"Yes, what's your name?"

The shadowy girl glanced around the basement, her gaze settling on a shelf above the washing machine. "Lye," she said.

"Lie? I'm not lying. I am Fiona. Who are you?"

"I am Lye. L-y-e. Lye is my name."

Fiona told her mother about her basement friend, to which her mother said, "That's nice. Wait until September and you will have real friends at school."

Now Lye glared at Fiona, shaking her head. So, Fiona stayed. The girl hoarded the toy plastic figurines Fiona had brought downstairs. When she asked to play with some of the toys, the girl buried the whole lot of them in the dirt. Fiona was only there to have dirt thrown at her face sometimes, it seemed. Lye laughed when she did that, and the laugh was so cold and strange. It sounded like it was made of the damp earth from which this friend had crawled.

"Fiona! Are you down there?"

Fiona shouted, "Yeah, I'm coming up now!"

Lye pushed Fiona, "Not a good friend!"

Fiona shrugged. "I have to, she knows I'm here. It's dinner time."

"Dinner time. Me, too."

"You can't. I don't think my mother would like you."

The shadowy girl leapt at her, hissing. That was the first time those long fingers reached out to scratch Fiona, catching her on the arm as she fled.

THE DOOR UNDER the lower balcony led to the basement hallway, with a door on the left to the tenant's basement area, a short flight of stairs on the right going up to the lower flat. The hallway continued about fifteen feet to the door that opened on the upper flat's basement. Fiona flicked all the lights on, but this did little to brighten the bleak route.

She started with large things, a broken chair, bags of moth-eaten winter coats, and her old snow sled. On her third trip back from the bin, she noticed the door to the tenant's basement was ajar. She paused, pondering if *stay out of my flat* also applied to the basement area, when the door opened wider and a little boy came out. He was about seven years old, with a mess of dirty blond hair hanging in his eyes. "Hi!" he said.

Fiona said, "Hello, do you live here?"

The boy nodded. "Wanna play trucks?"

Before Fiona could explain that *no, sorry I'm very busy*, the door to the lower flat opened and Mrs. Kavas called down, "Kevin, come upstairs now."

"But I'm gonna play with Fiona."

"No, leave her alone. Come up here."

Fiona took the lead up the steps, and Kevin followed. "Mrs.

Kavas, I didn't know you have a son . . . or grandson?" Fiona felt her face flush.

"Kevin is mine," Mrs. Kavas said, grabbing the boy's wrist and pulling him into the house. "I'll make sure he doesn't bother you anymore."

"It's no both—" The door slammed in Fiona's face.

Why so rude? What was she afraid of? Instead of going to collect the next load for the dumpster, Fiona walked into her tenant's basement. It was practically empty.

"HOW DID YOU scratch your arm? You know better than to touch your father's tools."

Fiona shook her head. "I didn't," she said. "Lye did this."

"You're not making any sense, but lie or no lie, I think you need to stop playing down there. It could be dangerous."

Fiona felt relieved. She couldn't help it if she wasn't *allowed* to play with Lye. That night she overheard her parents talking. "When are you going to fix that floor? Fiona gets covered in dirt almost every day down there in that hole."

"For crying out loud, just keep her up here. I'll get to it when I can. Why does she always go down there anyway?"

"She has an imaginary friend that lives in the basement."

Her parents laughed, but not Fiona. She truly wished Lye was imaginary.

Fiona thought she was in the clear, but the next day was laundry day. Her mother was not okay with leaving her alone upstairs, so to the basement she went again.

She wandered around, looking at all the old things her parents collected, just like she used to do. She tried on some old clothes, and played with an old set of dishes, but Lye shadowed her every move, hiding behind hanging laundry, or lurking in dim corners, until Fiona relented and sat once again in the dirt. If her mother happened to move toward the hole, Lye slithered under the dirt, out of sight.

When they were, at last, heading upstairs, her mother walked ahead. Before Fiona even reached the first step, Lye grabbed her arm. "Stay!"

Fiona screamed, "No, let go! Mommy, help me!"

Lye's fingers dug into Fiona's arm then swiped at her face, leaving a trail of bloody gouges. She pulled Fiona down, causing her to hit her head on the floor.

Her mother dropped the laundry basket, running back to her. "What on earth happened?"

Fiona stood up, crying, holding her head. She ran up the stairs, and in the kitchen told her mother everything about the shadowy girl from the dirt. Her mother said Fiona's imagination was going too far. That weekend, her father made time to repair the cement floor.

THE TENANT'S BASEMENT was surprisingly clean. There was a washer and dryer, some shelving holding laundry products, and a few storage bins. On the floor along one wall, three little metal trucks sat with an action figure. Kevin's toys. Then she saw there was a crack in the floor.

The memories flooded back. *It couldn't be*, she thought, yet she went to Mrs. Kavas's basement door and pounded.

"Are you a crazy lady? We're trying to eat here," Mrs. Kavas said, opening the door.

"I just wanted to let you know that the floor in your basement needs repair. I'll have someone patch the cement, as soon as I can—"

"Thought I told you to stay out of my unit?"

"The door was open; your son must have . . . anyway, as the owner of this house I have every right to enter both flats to make repairs."

"What if I don't want the floor repaired? I'm not paying for that."

"Don't worry, I'll pay for everything. Just don't let the boy down there. He could be in danger."

Mrs. Kavas laughed and again closed the door in Fiona's face, saying, "Danger from a crack in the floor? I think you might have a crack in your head!"

Fiona sat on the upstairs balcony with a cup of tea, as the sun set over the row of attached duplexes facing hers. She'd searched on her laptop for a contractor, but it was all too much: concrete companies, basement sealing companies, do-it-all handymen, and more. Now that she was trying to relax, it really wasn't working.

"Hey, up there, hello?"

Fiona looked down at the pathway in front of the house. A man stood there, looking up. "I've been ringing your bell. Come down please."

"Hi, who are you?"

She popped downstairs upon hearing it was Mr. Kavas. He wanted to be clear about not paying for any repairs. Fiona assured him he would not.

"I do have to get the house ready to sell, Mr. Kavas, so anything I see that needs fixing is going to be fixed. Let me know if there are any other problems. Any problems at all, like anything . . . unusual. Don't hesitate to tell me, please."

"Only other problem is, what happens to us? Are you going to kick us out?"

Fiona had never sold a house before, much less a duplex, and had not even considered the tenants. "Well, I'm sure whoever buys will rent out one or both units. I'm sure, since you always pay your rent, they'd be happy to keep you on."

"How much you selling for? I might—"

Kevin called from behind the door, "Daddy! You said you'd play games with us."

"Family calls," Mr. Kavas mumbled and disappeared inside.

Seeing Mr. Kavas made Fiona again question the couple having such a young son. She headed back upstairs to look for those rental papers.

The lease was signed by Harold and Joanne Kavas. Number of occupants listed: two. Pets: none, Children: none. Huh. Maybe her mother didn't bother with the details? Maybe the boy was born after—no, the latest agreement was signed only eight months ago.

Strange.

FIONA NEVER WENT down to the basement again from the day Lye attacked her to the day she left home at seventeen. Those years in between were filled with anger at her parents for not believing her and dread at the appearances Lye still seemed to make—usually in her bedroom in the middle of the night. Fiona never *saw* Lye again after her father patched the floor, but the bedroom visits brought harsh whispers and threats. She wanted Fiona to convince her parents to allow Lye upstairs.

Fiona resigned herself to the fact that she would never be believed, and she simply learned to live with it all. Lye visited but had to always go back to sleep in the basement floor. She tried to stay a whole day once, but she had begun to . . . "dry out," as she had whispered to Fiona, "like sand instead of the sweet dampness of my earthen lair—uh . . . my *home*."

Sometimes Fiona thought she did see Lye, in the form of a distorted shadow on the wall when the moon shone just right through her bedroom window. She told herself it was only a nightmare. When she occasionally woke with scratches on her legs, she doubted it was from anything but her own hands, scratching an itch in her sleep. When she heard her mother telling her father the basement floor needed repairs again, Fiona left home. She moved to the city where a friend's family had relocated and stayed with them to finish her final years of high school before starting college. She didn't go back, she found work, she made friends, and best of all she had escaped Lye. She even mostly forgot.

FIONA NOW SEARCHED for cement supplies. She could attempt to fix the cracked basement floor herself. It couldn't be that hard. She couldn't focus, though, her thoughts on the odd family living below her. It was almost ten o'clock—too late? Too bad . . . she found their telephone number on the rental agreement and dialed. Mr. Kavas answered.

"I know, I'm sorry, but I need to finish some paperwork here. Uh-huh, well it's about your son?"

She asked him about the lease, about the boy, even slyly bringing up their ages, and finally Mr. Kavas suggested they meet in the morning. *We can talk more, in private, without Kevin overhearing,* he said.

Fiona wanted to poke around the basement some more but was so leery of descending the spiral staircase of too many memories. She searched in a kitchen junk drawer for a flashlight, planning to go out the front door and down to the basement that way. She found a crumpled sheet of paper on top of the contents of the drawer. She smoothed it out and recognized her mother's handwriting:

I don't know what to think. Should I call her? Should I call the police? It is so difficult to explain. Like her, all those years ago, I think "Who will believe me!" But there is *evil here. There is evil living downstairs and I think it seeps up through the walls. I don't know what to do, I lay in my room at night but do not sleep. I try to leave the house for most of the day, but I am old. It is hard to go very far. Most of my good friends are dead. Should I call Fiona?*

The note was scrunched up in a ball and abandoned. The point was, she knew. Her mother knew about the darkness that came from the basement floor.

Fiona no longer felt compelled to visit the basement that night, but she found a flashlight anyway. She placed it on top of the junk mail on the bedside table, just in case. She slept, but not without dreams. She saw the basement as it was when she was a girl. She saw her mother's face covered with damp earth and gritty sand, and she saw Kevin standing over her bed, looking down through his mess of hair.

Nightmares, only nightmares, she thought upon waking in

the morning.

She was making breakfast when she heard a creaking sound behind her and turned from the stovetop to look. There was Kevin. The door to the basement staircase was wide open.

"Kevin! You scared me. What are you—"

"It's okay. I'm allowed."

Rather than *shoo* him off downstairs, Fiona realized this was an opportunity to gather information. She sat him at the table with a portion of her scrambled eggs and a slice of toast.

"Mmm, I love this kind of food," the boy said.

"Breakfast?"

He said nothing but munched away. He was wearing grey pajamas with a pattern of green dinosaurs. His hands looked grubby, the nails in need of a trim. Fiona sat beside him and reached a hand to his face. Kevin jerked back.

"Doesn't that hair bother your eyes?"

"No."

"Well, tell me something else, Kevin. When you're playing down in the basement, are you alone?"

"Yes. Except if Mommy or Daddy comes to play."

"In the basement?"

"Yeah, but they don't like it."

"How old are you, seven? Don't you go to school?"

"I am eight years old. Mommy knows I can't go to school. No outside."

Question time was over, because Kevin stood, said, "I'm going down the front stairs now!" and ran out of the kitchen.

"What? Wait, Kevin—"

He moved like a cat, disappearing around the corner at the

end of the hallway. Fiona found the door at the top of the front staircase open and took a step down. He was gone, and the door at the bottom was closed. She turned to go back into the hallway. That's when she felt the push.

A cry escaped her, but instinct kicked in and she grabbed the handrail as her face smashed into the stairwell wall and her shins banged against the wooden steps. She saw a figure dash out the door at the bottom, heard it slam. Kevin? Then she knew that her mother's deadly fall had not been an accident.

She rushed to the telephone, picked up the receiver, then slammed it back in its cradle. *What would she say?*

In the bathroom, checking her wounds, she found they were minor, but dabbed a bit of peroxide on a shin scratch. *That's what Mom used on my face the day Lye had attacked.*

She had to tell them what Kevin had done, so she went to the phone again. She could hear it ringing through the floor, but no one picked up. She realized Mr. Kavas would be waiting for her at the coffee shop down the street. She would tell him about Kevin and tell him everything about the dangers lurking in the basement.

The coffee shop was busy. There was no sign of Mr. Kavas. After ten minutes she walked back to the duplex and knocked on their door. No answer. She used her owner's key to unlock the door and entered the lower duplex.

Mr. Kavas was asleep on the couch, probably had an argument with his wife. She called to him, but he didn't stir. She checked the whole house. All the rooms were unoccupied, so to the basement she went.

Mrs. Kavas sat on the floor pushing a metal truck around.

Now dressed in a pair of shorts and a sleeveless shirt, Kevin sat on the crack—no, *in* the crack. It had split wider. Covered with dirt, bony knees sticking up from his crouched position as he scraped something through the grit, the resemblance was too much. Fiona knew that look. She felt sick to her stomach. To complete the vision, the boy finally pushed the hair off his face. The face was shadowy, hard to see, except for the eyes. They were bright aqua ringed with violet.

Kevin stood and laughed, dipping his face in a shy motion, and the dancing shadows became the face of Lye.

"Lye," Fiona said.

"Mrs. Kavas always wanted a boy. That's what she said to herself when she did her laundry. She cried for the little boy that never was . . ."

"Stop it! Kevin, you don't say any more!" Mrs. Kavas stood.

"Just like you wanted a little girl to play with, Fiona."

"Why do you come up here to torment us? Why?"

"Bored. No food down there, just souls and bugs. No toys."

In the dirt where Lye had crouched was a toy, Fiona's lost pony from all those years ago.

Mrs. Kavas was pale, blubbering, "I-I this boy just showed up. In my basement! He . . . called me Mommy and—"

Lye leapt up, hissing at Mrs. Kavas, and swiped at her with those long nails. "I like Fiona better than you."

Mrs. Kavas started bawling. "My Harold, he even took my Harold away."

"Your husband is upstairs, sleeping on the couch," Fiona said.

"Ohhh . . . " More crying.

"He would tell you everything," Lye said. "I pushed a cushion into his face. Weak lungs. Quick."

Backing toward the door, Fiona knew she had to get out of there. Lye was on her in a flash, those claws digging, digging in. Her legs wrapped around Fiona and her face was an inch away. Fiona saw what was beneath the shadows.

The creature's flesh was twisted ropes of mottled grey and green, covered with a shimmer of human skin. She struggled, moving across the basement until she was able to fling Lye away, and the thing crashed into the washing machine. Fiona stepped on its throat, holding it down. She reached for something from the shelf above the washer, a bottle with a big skull-and-crossbones warning sticker. She opened it and poured it into Lye's face. The irony was not lost on her when she noticed the product name. While the box in her mother's basement was crystals, this was liquid lye.

The thing screeched, an ancient guttural sound, and clawed at Fiona's foot and leg.

"Lye for Lye!" Fiona said.

The liquid caused the mottled skin to sizzle. Fiona poured some into its screaming mouth.

"Lye in the eye!" The bright aqua orbs melted away, revealing pure black eyeballs.

The thing groaned, hissing, *"Ssssisters, sissssters, brotherssss…"*

The bottle was empty. Fiona continued to press down on the creature, who still fought but was weak now.

"Why was it that Kevin couldn't go to school?" she shouted across the basement to Mrs. Kavas, who had collapsed against a wall, crying, and staring at the scene before her.

"Well, he . . . he was not like other boys."

"Why couldn't he go outside?!"

Through blubbering and tears, Mrs. Kavas passed on what Kevin had told her. The outside air hurt him. The sunlight, even moonlight was too strong, and he would turn to dust if exposed for more than a minute.

"Perfect. Now get over here and help me."

They carried Lye/Kevin/Thing out to the dumpster. The creature lay still, dying black eyes staring up. The body shriveled and became flaky. No doubt it would soon be dust.

Fiona descended the front staircase, carrying her suitcase, a bag of the few things she wanted from her mother's belongings, and a briefcase which held her laptop and papers.

Mrs. Kavas came out of her house. "What about me! What am I supposed to do? I can't stay here now!"

Fiona stopped on the pathway and looked at the woman. This woman who had brought back the thing from the earth, allowed it to kill her husband, *and* Fiona's mother. "Well Joanne, I'd say that's your damn problem!"

Driving up the street, Fiona had the briefcase open on the passenger seat. She pulled out a flyer from her mother's collection of junk mail.

His name was Fred and he wanted to buy *your* house. He would pay top dollar! Even carry out repairs and junk removal! No commission! Fred buys properties in any condition!

She would get only a fraction of what she would selling the house traditionally, but the house from hell would be out of her life. As she continued the drive out of town Fiona became increasingly aware that there were more than a few For Sale signs in the neighborhood, and quite a few contractor trucks parked in front of houses. The signs on the vehicles marked Driveway Repairs, Comfort Concrete, Mr. Handy General Contractors, Basement Flooring, and Cement Repair.

Fiona recalled the creature's final, desperate call:

"Ssssisters, sissssters, brothersssss."

LENE MACLEOD writes dark fiction and quiet horror in Ontario, Canada. Her debut collection, *Fringes of Grey*, has been published by DarkWinter Press. Publishing updates can be read on her website: www.lenemacleod.com.

A FOLDED LETTER

Neil Williamson

The crate, filthy and festooned with stamps and stapled customs dockets, blighted their tasteful suburban hallway. When Alasdair touched the thing, he found it horribly cold. As if it hadn't yet thawed from the weeks spent in a container on the deck of a monstrous ship, calling at who knew what benighted ports around the world before finally ending up here in England's gentle shires. In their hallway. Bare inches from Judy's prized rosewood telephone table. Indeed, it looked so damned out of place that Alasdair found himself unable to quite believe that *here* was where it ought to be. Yes, the address, wrapped in plastic and partially obscured by a boot print, appeared to be theirs but it had to be some sort of mistake, didn't it?

"Who was at the door at this hour?" Judy's voice called through from the back bedroom, sleep softened but also edged with concern.

Alasdair sighed. He'd hoped not to wake her. She needed the rest so badly. "Just a delivery," he said. "Go back to sleep." But he knew that was a futile wish.

"Well?" she persisted. "Who's it from then?"

Combing his fingers through his threadbare hair, Alasdair stared at what fishing in his admittedly shallow pool of knowledge looked to be Chinese characters stamped onto the battered wood.

"I've no idea," he called back, but that was only partly true because he had a foreboding. They only knew one person in the Far East, even if that person's name had long since fallen out of currency under this roof. He felt a twinge as something long-sunken worked itself loose from the floor of his memories, a stream of shameful bubbles trickling to the surface.

It couldn't really be her after all this time, could it?

Again, he attempted to resort to rationality—the whole thing had to be some ghastly cock-up—but it was no use. He needed to know. Judy was too much of an amateur Marple to be fobbed off by his evasiveness, but it would take her a few minutes to get herself into her chair and come through. He had time.

Retrieving his toolbox from the cupboard under the stairs, Alasdair knelt and slit the plastic ties. Then he prized open the lid and thrust his hand into the well of packing chips inside. His fingers quickly encountered two objects. They were solid and weighty, but otherwise were rendered indiscernible by thick layers of bubble wrap.

He heard Judy's wheels squeak on the kitchen linoleum. "Alasdair?" she called again. "What on Earth is it?"

"I'm trying to find out, love." His fingers closed at last around something recognizable and he pulled free a thick manila envelope possessing an unmistakable air of officialdom. There was a return address in the top corner for a firm of solicitors and notaries in Kowloon, and there was now no possibility of error because the name of Judy Hargreaves was printed right there in clear, bold type. Ripping open the envelope, Alasdair extracted a sheaf of legal-looking documents bound by rubber bands. He scanned the top page, a solicitor's letter, and was still trying to absorb the information it contained when something edged out of the sheaf. A much smaller envelope that had no place among the other documents. It was a precise and artful thing, and the sight of it stopped his heart because the name handwritten across it was not Judy's, but his own.

"What *is* it?" Judy said from the doorway. She couldn't come into the narrow hall itself. It had been the only part of their downstairs they'd been unable to modify after the chair became part of their lives. Alasdair surreptitiously slipped the smaller envelope into his dressing gown pocket before turning to his wife.

"It's Rosie Hyslop," he said, his voice thick with a cocktail of emotions, principal among them, he was ashamed to admit, relief. "It appears she's passed away. I'm so very sorry, my love."

He bent and embraced Judy, and then squeezed past her into the kitchen to put the kettle on as they began the business of finding out what had so unexpectedly been bequeathed by one long-estranged friend to the other.

The Lady Grey was tepid by the time Alasdair and Judy finished appraising the documents. The solicitor's letter, the report from the Coroner's Court, the copy of the will; although all of them were written in a dispassionate, unaffected English, the going had been slow as every detail of the surprising news gave rise to a new round of discussion. By mutual agreement, the bequests themselves were yet to be unwrapped. They sat on the counter between the kettle and the biscuit barrel; squat and obscure, even though the certificate of authenticity included among the documents described them quite plainly: *Foo Lion statues, glazed porcelain*, whatever those might be. It listed the maker and province too, with a date of manufacture that Alasdair thought immediately of as Victorian, but it wouldn't be, would it? That was English. It'd be some dynasty or other, although he really had no clue about all that stuff.

Through it all—the legal details, the discovery that Rosie had died as a consequence of alcoholism, poor thing, and that she had lived her last decade more or less in poverty—Alasdair stole glances at Judy, looking for signs as to how she was taking the news. She looked tired, but no more so than he'd become accustomed to during the gradual progression of her illness. There was certainly no outpouring of grief, though that had never been her style anyway. In times of trouble, Judy glazed over with an almost frightening calmness. Alasdair felt it best not to agitate her when she was in these moods, but he wondered now what she was thinking, under the surface. If she knew, perhaps even had *always* known, about . . . *the fling*, you couldn't call it an affair . . . he saw no sign of it. Her illness aside, the last two decades had been the most harmonious of their long marriage. He was as sure as he could be that there was no *jade elephant*, so to speak, in the room. They were so close that he would certainly have sensed it.

He cherished their life. The thought that something could jeopardize it was too awful to contemplate. And that was all it was, wasn't it? He was spooked by his own guilt over a misdeed now long in the past. There was no need to stir it up any further.

He remembered when he and Judy first met. She had been done up as a geisha. The party hadn't actually been a fancy dress one so, with the white makeup and the rosebud lips, the carefully arranged hair adorned with the red chrysanthemum that matched the ones patterning her kimono, Judy had rather stood out. *I'm an Orientalist*, she'd told him, her expression making it clear that she didn't care if he was impressed or not. He had been though. Found her dazzling amongst the conversational monotony of football and cars, skiing holidays and what was playing in the West End. So, instead of wrinkling his nose, he'd expressed interest.

He'd only discovered the true depths of her obsession with all things Asian when he was invited back to the flat on Old Milton Road. The phrase that came to mind as he took in the Hong Kong action and Japanese anime posters, the golden buddhas on the windowsills, the mats in the living room arranged around a low, square table, was *Aladdin's cave*. It didn't matter that the reference was to the Middle East, not the Far East. It was all *over there* somewhere, wasn't it? The girls' collection of exotic curios had been a hodgepodge of Saturday market tat, but their shared passion in decorating the flat had been obvious. Aspirational, a marker for bigger and better things. Even if those things were to prove in the long run to be different.

Alasdair and Judy had got on like a house on fire. When the flatmate, Rosie, had ghosted in with a dragon-patterned tea pot and some little cups it had felt like an intrusion. Rosie wasn't dressed up, only the lacquered chopsticks pinning her hair up a nod to the ubiquitous theme, and naturally Alasdair had assumed that she wasn't as much into the whole thing as Judy was. But he was wrong. Judy had been trying the Far East on like a costume, but the fanaticism for the East had coursed through her flatmate's veins. Rosie was saving up and would fly out to Tokyo a little over a year later, never to return to Good Old Blighty.

By contrast, when Judy and Alasdair had tumbled into bed that first night, their lovemaking had been wholeheartedly English. By the time they moved in together, Judy had all but put her flirtation with the exotic behind her.

"Well then," Alasdair said now, mustering a smile as he squared the documents back into their envelope. "Shall we see what we have?"

He didn't know why he was still nervous. How could some old knick-knacks possibly tell tales about something that had happened so long ago that it might as well never have? It was going to be fine.

It was probably considered absurdly insensitive to say *Aladdin's cave* these days, he thought distractedly as he set about peeling away the layers of bubble wrap. And *oriental* was a no-no too, wasn't it? It was such a minefield what you could and couldn't say now, with the PC police waiting to pounce and cancel you every time you opened your mouth. It was, as far as he was concerned, just one of a thousand reasons it was best to stick to British . . .

His train of thought juddered to a halt as the last of the wrapping fell away and revealed the first statuette in all its glory. That it was beautifully wrought was undeniable, the glaze a stunningly vivid shade of turquoise. But equally irrefutable was that the creature was hideous. Squatting on a square plinth, it had a flat nose, a mouth crammed with teeth, pointed ears and beady, black eyes. One of its taloned feet rested on a ball, making it look more like a dog than a lion, he thought. And with that, his sunken memories shifted again and a new stream of bubbles frothed to the surface.

They're called foo lions, foo dogs. Sometimes lion dogs? They're meant to guard your house from evil.

He remembered Rosie saying those words in a conversation arising from a less than complimentary remark he'd made about these very statues. He knew even as he began the mechanical motions of unwrapping the other one that it would be similar but instead of a ball it would have a cub by its feet. He hadn't twigged from the dry description, but now, yes, he remembered them. There had been one on the shelf by the front door of that cosy little Kyoto apartment, the other at the window, overlooking the noisy street below. He'd never quite been able to ignore its ugly shadow behind the blinds when they'd closed them for privacy.

"Well, there's nowhere to put them," Judy said, oblivious. "They won't go with anything."

Alasdair nodded, not trusting himself to speak quite yet, but glad to hear in her voice such a sensible opinion. Some years ago, the pair of them had got into antiquing, an activity that took them around the county, seeking out treasure in its many vintage shops and sale rooms. They were good at it. Of a single mind when it came to the selections they made. They'd even been on Bargain Hunt once, with only their expert's amateurish advice scuppering their chances of winning. Over the years, they'd turned their lovely home into a carefully curated assemblage of British elegance. She was right. There was certainly nowhere to put these statues where they would not stick out like two very blue, sore thumbs.

"Do you think they're valuable?"

"What?" he managed, still recovering from being confronted by these witnesses to his ancient infidelity.

"Well," she said, touching her earlobe thoughtfully, "I mean, leaving aside the question of *why* for a moment . . . "

"Why?"

She shot him an irritated look. "Yes, *why*. Why leave me these? It's not like we've been close in all the years since she went gallivanting. She never even hinted that she was ill in her emails."

Alasdair caught his breath. They'd kept in touch? How hadn't he known?

"But she knew I'd moved on from this kind of thing years ago," Judy continued, "so why would she imagine that I'd want these? For old times' sake?" Alasdair could only shrug. "Or did she finally go completely native? Did she actually believe I needed guarding? From what, Alasdair? From what?"

"I really couldn't say," he said, recognizing the rising note in her voice, and relieved to have a situation that he knew how to deal with. "I'll tell you what. I'll put them upstairs for now, shall I? And when I come back down, I'll tidy up all this mess and then make us a spot of lunch and we can see about getting them valued. We'll drop Marj from Treasure Hunters a line. She'll know who to ask about foreign stuff."

Judy offered him a thin smile. "That's a good idea, Alasdair. I apologize for shouting. It's all just . . . so unexpected."

"No trouble at all," he said, cradling one of the lions in the crook of his arm and reaching for the other.

"It wouldn't be terrible if they were worth a few bob, though," Judy said. "A nice gesture."

Such pragmatism was so typical of Judy that Alasdair almost laughed. But wait . . . was she really dismissing these gifts, or did she perhaps mean as *compensation*? For what he'd done? Did she know after all?

"They've got a certificate of authenticity, so that's . . . promising," he said hoarsely. "Back down in two ticks."

They'd never bothered to install a stair lift because it had been simpler to build an extension onto the dining room and convert it into a bedroom with an *en suite*. To all intents and purposes, they lived on the ground floor now, the upstairs bedrooms reserved as guest rooms. They were only really used for that though when Michelle and the kids flew over to visit and, since it was a long and expensive trip from New Brunswick, those rooms had come more and more to serve as storage space for pieces they hadn't quite found places for yet, as well as old ones that had fallen out of favor.

Alasdair dumped the ugly blue statues on an empty bookshelf. Even here they looked out of place. It wasn't just their luminosity next to his slowly growing collection of antique volumes. It was Hampshire's winter sunlight filtering through the blinds. These statues belonged under the warm, buttery sun of Japan. Here they were . . . misplaced, wrong.

Unreal.

ALASDAIR MANUFACTURED AN errand that afternoon. He hadn't been able to bring himself to open the letter from Rosie inside the house, not even upstairs. The guilt had continued to trickle steadily throughout the day. More than once he'd considered whether he ought to make a clean breast of the whole business and simply show Judy the letter. He'd even started wording an explanation. It would be painful, but their marriage was strong enough to absorb the damage, surely. It had been such a brief thing. A heat of the moment occurrence that had meant little to him at the time, and even less to Rosie. He'd thought about it so little since, it had become a fiction. Like something he'd watched on TV once rather than something he'd actually done.

He'd been a different person there.

It happened the year of the Japanese buy-out. Rowansons was still riding high, everyone believing they were stepping up onto the global stage. Alasdair hadn't even wanted to go. He'd already caught a whiff of the asset stripping rat that was lying in wait and, he'd discovered after a couple of disastrous package holidays, didn't particularly enjoy foreign travel anyway. In the end he'd given in because it offered an opportunity for Judy to visit the part of the world she'd once been so fascinated with, but she'd just been diagnosed and couldn't fly, so in the end he'd gone on his own.

Judy had said she wasn't fussed, though he'd always suspected she was putting on a brave face. She gave him Rosie's address in Kyoto—the latest port in her friend's erratic peregrination of the region—but Alasdair had no intention of looking her up. He'd barely known Rosie before she left and it was sure to be an awkward meeting without Judy there. He'd intended to excuse himself by saying that the schedule left no room for extracurricular arrangements, but in reality the opposite had turned out to be true. Left to his own devices, he'd struggled with the language, with the food and the summer humidity, with the strangeness of everything. So in the end, he'd rung her after all.

Seeing Kyoto through Rosie's eyes had been a revelation. He'd remembered her as reserved, but there she was effervescent, as if moving to the Far East had completed her in some fundamental way. She took his arm, like he was the old friend not Judy, and dragged him around tourist sites until his feet were sore, his ears too from her excitable chatter. It had been impossible not to be caught up by it.

The days that followed, Alasdair had for years chosen to suppress, but now moments returned to him in unbidden flashes. The mouth-watering aroma from the teppanyaki restaurant on the corner of her street. The feel of pliant tatami under his bare feet. The light, the air, the unfamiliar cadences of language and laughter. He remembered Rosie's sparky smile after they'd made love. It was the smile of a free spirit, and he'd mirrored it. Or perhaps the better word was *mimicked*.

On his last day, she'd given him a gift to take home to Judy, although he could not now recall what it had been. Something local and artisanal. Cheap, probably, but regardless it had been a deliberate gesture that drew a line under what they'd done together. Then she'd taken a square of paper, nimbly folded it into an origami crane and presented it to him along with a final kiss and the words: *Fly away home now.* Back in his hotel he'd slipped it between the pages of the paperback he'd bought for the plane, but when they had touched down at Heathrow he'd deliberately left the book in the seat pocket.

Standing now outside the village Co-op, his fingers shook as he opened the precise little envelope. He was not the least surprised to discover the contents to be a thing of simple, artful angles. A paper crane.

Once unfolded, Alasdair found Rosie's letter to be short. Even reading it for a third time he could not say he felt better, although there was nothing damning *per se* in her otherwise no-more-than-friendly reminiscence of his visit.

But there were these lines: *I always felt it such a shame that Judy was unable to join us. It would have been better if she had. I wanted her to follow her heart and come out much earlier, of course. Did she tell you that? It was so unfair that she couldn't. So unfair.*

Alasdair didn't know what to make of it. It wasn't an accusation exactly, it wasn't even… He yelped with pain. Sucked the pad of his finger, suddenly afire from the paper cut incurred as he'd tried to stuff the letter back into its envelope. He shook his throbbing hand. Unable to believe that such an inconsequential thing could hurt so damn much.

He had been fearful before, but now he was angry. Even in death Rosie was finding a way to intrude, and it was wholly unnecessary.

This, he determined, was the end of it.

THEY PASSED THE evening in their usual fashion. Alasdair roasted a Waitrose chicken and opened a bottle of Liebfraumilch from the case that one of his old clients sent them for Christmas.

"Oh, you've made real gravy!" Judy said, and then frowned, suspicious. "What have you done?"

Of course, she was joking, but it jarred that her immediate response on noticing that he'd gone to a little extra effort instead of resorting to slumming it with the usual Bisto granules was to imply that he was trying to make amends for something.

"Oh, nothing a dustpan and brush won't fix," he made himself joke back, sounding far more casual than he felt. "Honestly, you've so much Clarice upstairs, it's not like you'll notice one piece fewer."

"You'd better be kidding." She said it with a smile, but one he was entirely unable to interpret.

They watched *Flog It* while they ate, and then switched to an old Morse on ITV3. As Alasdair began to clear away the dinner things, he blurted, "So what did you talk about in your emails?"

"Hmm?" Judy looked up from her Word Search. She wasn't paying attention to the show, they'd seen them all so many times. It was just nice to have it on. The worsted wool and real ale. "What emails?"

"With Rosie." He was committed now and, damn it, he did want to know. "Didn't you say you were in contact?"

"Oh..." Her expression clouded. "Well, nothing much really, just chit-chat. Catching up, you know? What was going on here, what life was like in Japan or Hong Kong or wherever she happened to be at the time. It started off as Christmases and birthdays, but eventually it was just whenever we got around to it." She shrugged.

"Oh," he said and, even though he burned to know what had passed between them about life in Japan, he clamped his lips shut and went back to watching John Thaw pontificating over his pint of bitter. His concentration, though, was as much in smithereens as the imagined Clarice Cliff he'd joked about earlier. Not knowing Judy's thoughts was driving him to distraction. Could she be waiting for him to come clean? She always said that an apology meant more when it was offered rather than surrendered, didn't she? Absentmindedly, he sucked the pad of his finger. The damned thing still stung.

Alasdair watched Judy out of the corner of his eye. Her face was a mask of concentration. One half bathed in the television flicker, the other in the pretty multi-hued glow of the Tiffany lamp by her elbow. All of her, from the loose, greying wisp at her brow, to the horn-rimmed spectacles through which she peered at her puzzle magazine, to the Parker pen with which she drew precise circles around the letters, was so very English. His English Rose, was how he always thought of her. Privately anyway, he'd never said it out loud . . . probably, he realized now, because of the obvious similarity to the name of the woman he'd lain with out of wedlock . . .

Lain with? Out of wedlock?

He couldn't even articulate the truth to himself.

The woman. He'd. Fucked. And who'd fucked him for five glorious, ravenous, sweat-sodden days and nights. Who'd opened his eyes to the possibility of a life so very different to the tidy, tea-and-toast one that he and Judy were cultivating back in the Shires. Not *offered* it to him, just showed him that it existed, and then whipped it away again.

I wanted her to follow her heart, Rosie had written in her letter to him, and he wondered now if he was meant to have felt spurned instead of relieved when he'd got on that plane. Was that what it had been, their dalliance? A rebuke for turning Judy's head away from the Grand Plan? Or was it really just as it had seemed on the surface: an innocent piece of unplanned fun. No strings, guilt-free.

Alasdair didn't believe in those. The trickle of guilt, now released after so long, had become an undammable stream.

IT TOOK ALASDAIR forever to fall asleep that night. He helped Judy wash and dress for bed and then tucked her in before climbing into his own narrow single bed on the opposite side of the room. Then he lay there, listening. His own hammering pulse so loud in his ears that he could barely hear her breathing. Couldn't tell if she was asleep yet or was lying awake too. If angry thoughts might be running hot behind her closed eyelids. Long coddled suspicions about what had really happened on that long ago trip from which she had been excluded. Even if she had no such suspicions, could those damn statues have disinterred Judy's youthful dreams, as they had Alasdair's guilt? Was she even now sifting through the detritus, wondering about what might have been?

Alasdair stared at the shadow-patterned ceiling and remembered Judy as he'd first met her. How exciting she'd been, but also, how innocent and malleable. Then he imagined her and Rosie out in the city on a humid evening. Eating okonomiyaki in that little place in the mall. Drinking shots of Suntory and teasing the local men in one of those narrow bars, her eyes bright and wild. The glisten on her pink skin later when she took one of them home. A different one every night perhaps since she was free to do anything she wanted. He imagined her laughing. Proper laughing, brash and full of unrestrained joy. He couldn't remember the last time anyone had laughed like that in this house.

The more he imagined, the less he could believe *that* Judy could exist here. In England, in this house, in the bed across the room. Its covers looked flat from here, didn't they? Empty.

Which was ridiculous, he told himself. *Madness.* Of course, she was there, just as she had been every single night of the last twenty-seven years. She was there and she loved him. She *depended* on him. All this was just him holding his own head under a gushing torrent of fetid guilt. Maybe he even deserved it, but this was enough now. *Enough.* Things happened in life, people made choices. Not every road not taken was a wasted opportunity. Theirs was a good life, and they were happy.

All he needed to do to prove it was raise his head and see her lying there asleep, a smile on her peaceful lips. But he could not make himself look. What if he couldn't tell peace from glaze?

Alasdair stared at the ceiling. At the overlapping shadows, sharp and geometric. That shivered, and then quaked, and then broke apart into a thousand fluttering angles, that wheeled and twisted, that melded and broke apart again like a murmuration.

There was a sound. The whisper and snap of paper.

He opened his eyes. They were gluey from sleep, his thoughts groggy and confused. There was a figure, he thought, standing over him. "Judy?" he murmured. "Is it you?"

But no. How could it be her? How could she be standing? Anyway, this figure was too large to be Judy. In outline, too regular, too . . . *straight*. Once again, the stillness exploded into flurry and chaos. Reflexively, Alasdair shut his eyes, but he felt the wind of it on his face. It went on for long seconds. But eventually everything was still again.

This time he knew—*just knew, without question*—that he was alone in the room. And when he finally sat up and looked over to Judy's bed he was proved right.

Alasdair got out of bed and put on his dressing gown. Her chair was still there, he noted, but the duvet had been thrown onto the floor. The door of the bathroom was open and, though the light was off, he could see that it was empty too.

"Judy?" In the hall, his shout fell flat and lifeless. When he tried again in the empty kitchen it came out choked. "Jude?"

It only took a few minutes to ascertain that his wife was nowhere on the ground floor. And so now he stood beside the elegant English rosewood telephone table at the foot of the stairs, looking up . . . at the buttery daylight spilling out of an upstairs bedroom. At the bright turquoise of the two snarling statues that had found their way to the top step.

"No!" He began climbing.

With each step came another new memory. The delicious aroma of plum wine. The hubbub of foreign conversation in a busy café. A long silver peal of laughter. Judy's laughter. In a different world.

"No," he said again, taking the stairs two at a time. "Judy? Jude!"

Someone came out of the room. *Something.* Stalking stiffly, wings outstretched, beak grazing the carpet. All angles and blades and deadly intent.

Alasdair stopped a couple of steps from the top. His face inches from the hooked crease of its beak. "No," he whispered.

The bedroom door banged shut, the beautiful light extinguished. The folded crane lunged. Alasdair swayed. It exploded into a storm of whirling whispers. He stumbled. He fell.

Lying at the bottom of the stairs, he knew that he would be bruised for weeks but he didn't think anything was broken. His injuries from the fall, however, were not the source of the severest pain.

It was the cuts covering his hands and arms and face. Fine, but oh so deep. Every one a reminder of where she had gone. It was the not knowing when, or even if, she would return. It was hurt everlasting.

Which, he realized, was precisely as it ought to be.

NEIL WILLIAMSON lives in Glasgow, Scotland. His work has been shortlisted for British Science Fiction Association, British Fantasy and World Fantasy awards, and his most recent book is the urban folk horror novella, *Charlie Says*. "A Folded Letter" is the latest in a sequence of tales of weird bequests and inheritances. Previous instalments have appeared in *Black Static*, *The Dark*, *Weird Horror*, *Interzone Digital* and *Best Horror of the Year*.

DR. FULLER'S LAST LECTURE

Logan McConnell

M att snaked his way through a maze of mansions and iron gates, addresses obscured in the pitch black. The night's rolling blackout had blotted the town, casting him into darkness. Eventually he found his destination and wandered uphill to the home of Dr. H. M. Fuller, Ph.D.

Matt knocked. A shuffle of footsteps stirred inside, the sound of creaking floorboards growing closer until they ended with a slow swing of the front door. Matt recognized his biochemistry professor in the dark by his lanky, six-five silhouette towering in the doorway.

Even without lights, Matt could sense all of Fuller's minuscule peculiarities. The doctor's breathing was a beat too slow, his posture too crooked, his stare a bit too intense in any given situation. Fuller always struck Matt as a visitor from some secret parallel life, one that mimicked humankind imperfectly with a forgery that was only close to convincing.

Yet Matt worked around his own sense of unease. Fuller's brilliance was a well-kept secret in the university. His unassuming basement office was tucked under layers of concrete where he remained a quiet giant keeping to himself, teaching esoteric electives for biochem majors.

Fuller was Matt's professor for one of these classes, and after a disastrous midterm Matt reached out to Fuller. The student fretted over his failing grades and Fuller offered Matt private tutoring, with fantastic results.

In time, the two agreed to collaborate on a research project, Fuller insisting they discuss details at his home. Matt didn't want to go. Teacher-student outings weren't unheard of—bonding over beers in bars occurred now and then—but Fuller's offer was surprising. He didn't seem like the type to host guests, at least not voluntarily. Fuller lived with an aversion to attention, inviting few to glimpse his private world. Yet here Matt stood, at its threshold.

"Matt, Matt, Matt," said Fuller. "Glad you found the place. Please come in."

Matt entered. Finding no flashlight or candles, he reached for his phone to light the way.

"Ah-ah! No gadgets," Fuller sang. "We stare at screens all day, let's take a break from them, yes?"

Matt slipped his phone back into his pocket. He stretched his arms out on either side, slamming his fingertips into wooden walls. What he thought to be a wide entryway was in fact a narrow hall.

"Dr. Fuller, I may need you to lead the way, not exactly sure where to go," said Matt, careful not to sound too demanding.

Fuller shut the front door. "Nonsense young man, you're sharp as a tack. Surely you don't need help. Go ahead and find your way to the living room. First doorway on your right."

Matt had learned to expect this kind of odd prompting from Fuller. He had a predilection for turning mundane tasks into quirky puzzles, testing Matt's intellect as well as patience. Matt never knew if this was from some belief by Fuller that solving riddles built character, or if these moments were outlets for a hidden sadism lurking deep within. Not wanting to argue, Matt complied.

Tapping feet eased Matt deeper into the house, slowly inching his way down the hall while Fuller kept close by. Further in, Matt saw a room to his left. Distant starlight through an open window faintly illuminated various furniture outlines in the room. A fat armchair sat beside a lamp, adorned with lumps and uneven curves Matt guessed to be ornate decorations.

"The library," said Fuller, as if reading Matt's mind.

Matt continued, feeling the left wall reappear then vanish again, discovering another room, also with open windows. A table's outline dominated the room's center, its underbelly hidden in shadow except for a corner leg, the end carved to resemble a clenched fist. The far wall wasn't touched by starlight, remaining unseen, as if the furniture sat within a vast, endless space.

"Dining room," Fuller said, casually.

The furniture in both rooms were appropriate sizes but with warped dimensions. Lengths and widths were out of sync, lines and edges rolling sinews instead of blocks with perfect angles as the borders. Each piece was similar to but not exactly what Matt expected: a table-esque blob next to a lamp-like thing between two chair-ish squares.

Matt felt an entrance on his right. He breathed and relaxed his shoulders; the game was finally over. Inside the living room the windows were covered, shrouding the room in a total darkness that made the previous areas look bright by comparison.

"Dr. Fuller, I really think I'll need my phone, or a flashlight or something. I can't see anything."

"Nonsense! You're so close to the couch. Come along now, almost there."

Matt could see nothing as he moved forward. His nerves tensed in anticipation of stubbing a toe on a television stand or thudding his head against a ceiling fan. His shins brushed past what he thought to be the plush of a footrest, and followed its soft edges to discover a couch close by. He sat.

The seat's creaking announced to Fuller that Matt had found the desired spot. "Outstanding, young man. Good work," said Fuller, whose voice hovered around Matt before landing in an adjacent place, likely a loveseat. He heard two soft thuds he assumed was Fuller utilizing the footrest between them.

Settling in, Matt sniffed the air. The scent of chamomile tickled his nose.

"In front of you," said Fuller, "on the table, is a cup of tea, if you're so inclined."

Matt reached out and found the handle. He sipped loudly to indicate he had accepted Fuller's hospitality.

"Thank you, it's quite nice." Matt set the cup down. "I bet the power will return soon. I'd like to actually see your place," he said.

"I'd like you to see it too, Matt."

Matt leaned back. "Are you sure you don't want some lights on? I've got a flashlight on my phone," he offered.

"I'm quite comfortable in the dark. Have been ever since college. Actually, Matt, did I ever tell you how I got into biochemistry?"

Matt shook his head. He then realized Fuller couldn't see him, and said, "Uh, no, you haven't."

"I initially started college as a biology major, with an interest in birds. One summer I was selected to join a research team. We flew to central Europe to observe behavior patterns of the great bustard. Am I correct in assuming you've never heard of the great bustard?"

Baffled by this visit's beginning, and where Fuller's story was leading, Matt uttered a polite, "No. I mean, yes, you are correct I've not heard of them."

"That's expected. They aren't native to North America. The great bustard is one of the largest birds in the world. It sets the record for the heaviest bird on Earth that can still fly. Fascinating creatures, really.

"Only one other undergraduate student was picked to go on this little adventure. We'll call her Kate. That wasn't her name but for the story's sake let's go with Kate. Kate and I were up early one morning, assigned by our professor to observe the great bustards out in the fields: record their mating calls, when they ate, things of that nature.

"Of course, we had to get close to the birds. So, how to go about that? Humans startle them, you see. Well, Kate and I donned these tarp gowns, a camouflage of sorts, allowing us to creep up and study the great bustards without their notice. We spent our time documenting their habits day after day, all summer long, until we had enough to publish a research paper in some obscure ornithology journal that is now out of print. So goes academia.

"Now Matt . . . " Fuller stopped, clicked his tongue, and shifted to the tone of voice he used when lecturing. "Can you tell me, what about that summer was the most fascinating? What was *really* important? I'll give you a hint: it wasn't the great bustard."

Absent of answers, Matt bought time with a long sip of tea. The professor was behaving more playful than usual, stretching his game of annoying questions to a much longer duration. But Matt needed to get published. He needed Fuller.

Matt whispered, "Research experience?" hoping this would redirect their talks to Matt's preferred topic.

"No, no. Take another guess."

Matt sighed. "Was it Kate? Did she become a friend or something?"

"Nope. It was the tarp. The tarp gown I mentioned. Our professor had a name for it: Dehumanization Suit."

Fuller spoke the word slowly as if to savor it, like each letter was a delicious treat.

"De-hum-an-iz-ation Suit," he repeated. "Kate put hers on first. That face of hers, her eyes, her lips, her body, all slipped away before me. I watched an actual human devolve into a matted clump of cloth."

Fuller took a deep breath, held it for several seconds, then exhaled. Then again. Matt sensed Fuller was reliving that moment in his mind, trying to smell the odor of the suit, visualize "Kate" step inside its confines. He was sharing a sacred corner of his memory with Matt, a formative fragment of time that forever altered his life.

Matt sat up straight, creaking the couch.

"I didn't understand it at the time, Matt. I didn't understand what about this was so interesting, what was so . . . exciting. Every morning, I shook in anticipation of that precious process where Kate's transformation would begin again.

"Though, before I knew it, summer was over. Back to the States, back to class, those exhilarating moments over, or so I thought. I never stopped thinking about that dehumanization suit. I purchased one and hid it in my dorm, under the mattress, just in case a volunteer to wear it should pass my way.

"Fast forward to my junior year, when I found myself flipping through a magazine, a local one that was a bit risqué. It was filled with advertisements for certain sexual services and such, but I only looked because I was bored. I'm no deviant."

Fuller stopped, the silence striking Matt as an opening to affirm Fuller's claim and continue without judgment. Matt muttered, "OK."

"Glad you understand. So, in this magazine there was an advertisement placed by a woman who described herself as a masochist. I suspect you're familiar with the term. Now, that kind of crowd isn't to my liking. Yet something about her advertisement captured my attention.

"This was a woman, 24 years old, looking for discreet fun with a man who would dominate her. Under her interests were all manner of distasteful things: handcuffs, rope, paddles, humiliation, pain, blah, blah, blah. Strangely enough, she also listed that she could be used as a human footstool.

"A footstool . . . she *wanted* to be dehumanized, which I was only too happy to oblige. I truly believed that she would agree to wear the tarp. In hindsight, what I was looking for is colloquially referred to as a gimp, by the members of such circles, but I didn't know that at the time. All I knew was I had found someone willing to swap their humanity for an impersonation of the inanimate."

Matt was ready to bolt out of the house. This story was veering off into sexual dalliances he'd prefer not to know about. He tried to speak up, but Fuller cut him off and continued.

"I contacted the girl, claiming to be an experienced member of this freakish community, and invited her over with promises to fulfill her every fantasy, discreetly, so as to not damage her reputation. When she arrived, I failed to mask my eagerness, and blurted out that we should start by making her my footstool. She agreed.

"I pulled out my dehumanization suit and insisted she wear it, but she refused. Now how did she expect me to picture someone as an object with their entire head exposed? But I digress. As it turned out, she didn't ruin my night in the least. Very much the trooper, she kept to her role as footstool, bare knees against my hardwood floors for fifteen minutes without moving.

"That quarter hour was ... eye opening. I discovered having her there without the suit made my experience all the better. Seeing a human serve in an inhuman fashion, to bear a face as blank as upholstered wood, that woman straddled the barrier between living and nonliving, existing as neither but also both all at once. The feeling is just ... ah ... "

Fuller's words drifted away once again. Matt thought for a moment he could hear the doctor's heart fluttering like a soft drumbeat in the darkness, pulsating in the ecstasy of his reverie.

"Dr. Fuller, perhaps we could talk about some research ideas you had? I was thinking we could—"

"Matthew," said Fuller, "this *is* a discussion about research. You can't properly understand my proposal without hearing this information. Think of what I'm telling you now as the beginning of our study, an abstract, all right? Relax. Enjoy your tea and hear me out. I promise this is all going somewhere."

Feeling again for the tea, the beverage now room temperature, Matt finished what was left in one gulp.

"Where was I? Oh yes, that woman didn't come back again. What I saw as the main course of the evening—her being a footstool—she considered an appetizer, so to speak. Meaning, this degenerate actually wanted to stop being furniture and start being tied up, hit, and finish with sex! Yes, Matthew, it's a crazy world indeed.

"I put my own ad in that dirty magazine. I used a term I had recently discovered. The term I used was: Forniphilia. Have you heard of forniphilia, Matthew?"

"N . . . no."

"Forniphilia is a kink, a desire to be human furniture. If you ever find forniphilia photography, you'll see large tables made from intricate matrices of folded bodies. Lattices of people piles composing couches and bookshelves. Really remarkable. Well, by luck, someone answered my ad.

"It was a meek fellow, a gay man—no judgment, to his or her own—and he was exactly what I was after. He didn't want the flashy lewd gimmicks of my female footstool, no, he longed to be ignored. He would probably be gung-ho to don the dehumanization suit, though by then I understood it was better without coverings, to clearly observe the juxtaposition of person and thing uniting as one.

"Our first night together, I had him crouch in a corner, and act like he was a table with a beautiful vase on top, one that would fall and shatter should he move. Other nights he'd pretend to be a chair, then a lamp, once even a fridge! Obviously, he didn't function as an actual refrigerator, but we would mime out the actions, opening his 'door' and such. All the while his eyes were stuck in a fixed stare, unflinching, like glass ornaments encased in marble."

Fuller stopped and sighed. Matt tensed, then turned to look around, searching for any light to guide him back to the hallway. Shuffling to the other end of the couch, all he saw was soft starlight through the dining room window from across the hall. Matt's eyes locked onto the table leg he had seen earlier, a decorative fist with fingers pressed into the carpet. He noticed a soft pink hue around the knuckles.

Matt stood. Fuller continued talking about his niche fetish

of blending furniture and flesh as Matt silently moved towards the hall, through the void of the living room. His legs were heavy, feet like anchors shuffling painfully slow. Matt leaned forward and pressed against some item that felt like a mix between a bureau and an elbow.

He pulled his phone from his pocket, stunned to find it too heavy to hold. Matt managed to press his thumb against the side, shining light before dropping the device from his grasp. As his phone fell, the lit screen twirled in blackness, revealing dozens of frozen eyes, all dispersed around the living room before striking the floor face down.

"Are we alone?" Matt asked, slurring his words.

"Ah, you're trying to leave. Matt, I didn't peg you as the inpatient type, but no matter. I will cut to the chase. My explorations went deeper and deeper. At times, I thought myself afflicted with a kink of my own, though I never derived any carnal gratification from this activity.

"I found a small number of people who wish to be objects, who wish to be used. Of course, I keep some real furniture around for the sake of comfort, such as the couch you were sitting on tonight. But for those people who fantasized about being dehumanized, I made their wish come true.

"That may sound strange to you, but there is a peace achieved in this blissful state. How much anguish is thrust upon you, Matt, stressing over your research? Your exam grades? Impressing others? Being different versions of yourself to different people throughout the day?

"But a chair is a chair. A lamp is a lamp. There's a Zen-like tranquility in being only one thing, an equanimity in becoming a singular, constant formation. Furniture completes its purpose by simply existing. Exist here, with me, in the dark. The darkness wraps over you, shields you like a womb. No more rushing through a blur of traffic, no more hustling through campus, the never-ending kaleidoscopic swirl of nightmarish obligations is over.

"Instead, exist with the others I've saved. An anxious, bookish man is now a shelf in my library. A fat, lonely woman who simply wanted to cuddle, is now a splendid armchair. A failed actress, suffering in the gutters of Hollywood Boulevard, is now a lamp, the spotlight she so desperately sought forever in her hands.

"How do they achieve this freedom? Biochemistry! See Matthew, I'm a man of my word. Told you I'd get around to it. I've created a beautiful concoction to freeze a person, so to speak. Slow their metabolism and cardiovascular system and even consciousness to a speed barely above death. Their muscles maintain what's called a waxy rigidity, so I can twist them into different angles. Well, that was in your tea tonight.

"Your body will begin to slow now. So will your thoughts. Did you know everyone has an inner monologue in their mind? Some constant narration that blended into your psyche's background long ago, existing without notice. That will fade next. I'm sure it was working in overdrive tonight, blabbering things like, 'Matt drove through the dark hills,' or 'Matt began to worry about weird Dr. Fuller.' That part of you will be hushed soon. Go ahead, try and think thoughts like that now.

"See? You can't. And thank goodness, all that rumination and worry is now silenced. You're welcome, Matt. Hm . . . *Matt*

Even the name is perfect. You have the same name as an object, did you ever think of that? So easy to please, so willing to cater to others, I had you down as a doormat at first, though on second thought you'd be too lumpy. Don't worry, I'll find a place for you here, inside my little furniture zoo. Perhaps a coat rack?

"Though, Matt, or Coat Rack, I do have to unburden myself. I do have to share with you one more secret while you can still process language. Something awful happened. A while back I went on a shopping spree, going through alleys and homeless shelters looking to furnish my home with new furniture. I brought them all back here, with promises of food and shelter.

"I gave them the same tea as you, the same speech I've given you to ease them into their new state, aligned their still frames into their assigned shapes, and placed them beside their new brothers and sisters. But I do confess, I made a bad batch of tea. I was not the best biochemist in those early days. It succeeded in freezing their muscles forever, but not their minds. That was temporary.

"In the middle of the night, while I slept, they 'woke up'. The batch wore off, on their consciousness, at least. My house was filled with muffled screams. A few managed to move their lips. They said things to me, Coat Rack, awful things. I thought it was a horrible dream, stumbling in pitch black as they yelled bloodcurdling cries, every corner of the house an echo chamber of agony without end. I almost went mad.

"Do you know how difficult that was for me? Pouring more tea into my furniture? Well, the second batch was perfect, thank goodness. No more screams. And I swear, Coat Rack, I'll do my best to make sure that never happens to you. I promise.

I'll take care of you, keep you happy in that quiet twilight between wake and sleep, human and thing.

"But . . . if you do awake, promise you won't scream? Promise you'll only whisper, Coat Rack."

LOGAN MCCONNELL is a horror writer living with his husband in Tennessee. He spends his free time taking long walks in the woods and sitting alone in the dark. His work is published or upcoming in *Cosmic Horror Monthly*, *Coffin Bell*, *Dark Recesses Press*, *Archive of the Odd*, *Lovecraftiana* and others. Twitter: @LMwriter91

WILD PLACES

Tim Jeffreys

I'd had a bad feeling about the trip from the beginning. When Luis first showed me those photographs Theodore Munroe took deep in the woods in northern Spain, a shiver passed through me. An uneasy feeling stayed with me for days after. Then when Luis told me he was to join one of Munroe's expeditions, returning to that place where the photographs were taken, working undercover for *Features* magazine, I did everything I could to convince him not to go. I don't even know why I was so against the idea; I just couldn't shake the dread those pictures instilled in me. But it was no use.

Luis had made up his mind. *Features* wanted him to expose Munroe as a fraud, and I think something in Luis relished that idea. Or perhaps, like me, he just knew he'd sleep a damn sight easier knowing those photographs were faked.

Seeing my husband step through the airport Arrivals gate, looking bruised and forlorn with one arm in plaster and a long cut held together by stitches on his forehead, I could no longer deny that something awful had happened in Spain. I knew this already, of course, because I'd caught snatches on the news. Most of his expedition party had vanished, including Munroe himself, and some Hollywood actor. But I'd been in the sleep-deprived fug that comes with having a newborn, and once Luis called to say he'd made it out I just got on with attending to the baby. But I could tell by the way Luis held onto me when we hugged that the experience had left him with more than physical scars. Luis didn't rattle easily, but he was shaken, I could tell, and I was shocked to see him that way.

"Where is she?" he said, chocking back tears when at last he let me go. "Where's my baby girl?"

"She's with my mother," I told him. "Mum's been staying with me at the house." Pulling back, I examined his face. "What? What is it?"

He shook his head. "Not now. Now, I just want to go home."

It was dark when we left the airport, with a chill in the air which surprised me. It seemed only a week or so ago we'd been battling a heat wave. The air had that fresh, indescribable smell of autumn. We walked to the car park in silence. I held on to Luis' hand and could feel it trembling. I wanted desperately to ask about the trip, about the missing people, about the Spanish men who'd beat him up and put him in hospital after he returned from the woods. But something stopped me. Luis seemed so unlike himself, so internalized, that it was like walking beside a stranger.

Then he looked at me and smiled, and I saw a flicker of the old Luis. The man I first encountered when he had root canal treatment at the dental clinic where I worked on reception; but hadn't let that stop him asking me out on a date.

"I can't wait to hold her in my arms, Siobhan," he said. "Our daughter. My God—she doesn't even have a name yet, does she?"

"I'm leaning towards Holly," I told him.

"Holly? Yes, I like that. Holly."

"She has your eyes. She's gorgeous, Luis. A little angel." I squeezed his hand. "You wait and see."

"I'll bet."

It slipped out then as we entered the car-park, though I did my best to keep my voice casual. "So . . . do you think they'll find them? Theodore Munroe, and the others?" I tried to remember the name of the Hollywood actor who'd also vanished. Black somebody. Wilder Black? He'd been a child star in the 80s, according to the news reports, but being a nineties kid I'd never heard of him.

Luis shook his head. "Munroe's dead."

I gasped, shocked by the matter-of-fact way he said this, and stared at him. "Dead? How can you be so sure? They might still . . ."

"He's dead, Siobhan. I saw his body. Or rather . . ." He grimaced. " . . . what was left of it."

"What're you saying?"

He stopped walking and faced me. "I'm saying . . . " He glanced around as if he thought someone might be listening, although we were alone. " . . . something in those woods tore Munroe to pieces."

"What?"

"And the others . . . the ones that are missing. They're all dead too. I'm sure of it."

"*Jesus*. But . . . what was it? What did that?"

He was silent a moment, his lips pressed together. Then, after glancing around again, he urged me to start walking. "I don't think we should talk about it," he said. "Not ever."

"But . . . "

"I think we should just forget it."

AND SO THAT'S what I tried to do. Forget about it. Not that hard when you're sleep-deprived and have a month-old baby keeping you busy around the clock. When I wasn't feeding Holly, or changing Holly, or pushing Holly around the local park in her pram, navigating sodden piles of fallen leaves, I was trying to catch up on sleep or grabbing a bite to eat. There was comfort in that, of letting the world fade into the background while I concentrated on that one task, the task of caring for my baby.

Still, it was tough at times. Holly had colic, and would cry for what seemed like hours after a feed until my nerves were in shreds. Thank God for Mum, because Luis wasn't much help. In the first few weeks after his return, he got even less sleep than I did, and not only because of the baby. He'd started having nightmares. One night he woke up everyone in the house, shouting. Said he'd dreamed that vines and branches had burst up through the mattress and wrapped around him, entwining him and pulling him down into the bed. Poor Mum looked terrified. As much as I wanted to sympathize, I couldn't help being short with him. It had taken me more than an hour to get Holly settled that evening and I hadn't long climbed into bed when he started hollering.

"You have to snap out of it, Luis," I told him after I got Holly down and Mum returned to bed. "I need you. Mum won't be here forever, and I can't do this all on my own. I . . . "

I caught myself, aware of some shift in the dynamic of our relationship. I'd never had to speak to him that way before. He'd always been the strong one. The one who led. He's more than a decade older than me, after all, an experienced journalist who often worked undercover on a story, and spoke three languages. And there's me, the dental receptionist not quite out of her twenties, telling him off as if he was a child.

It felt odd. Uncomfortable. I wondered: would I have to be the strong one now?

He sat slumped forward in the chair, his head in his hands.

"I'm sorry, Siobhan. I don't know what's wrong with me. I don't."

Calming, I rubbed his back with one hand. "Maybe you need to talk with someone. What you saw in Spain. What happened in those woods. I know you said we should try to forget it, but it's eating you up. You could have PTSD or something."

He lifted his head. "PTSD?"

"You don't go through an experience like that, seeing people killed—pulled to bits, you said—without it affecting you.

You need to talk to someone."

He shook his head. "I can't ever talk about it. To anyone." Gingerly, he touched the wound on his forehead. He'd recently had the stitches removed but it had not yet fully healed.

"You need help, Luis."

"No. No." Brushing me off, he left the kitchen. I followed him into the hall and saw him go into the lounge. He left the lights off. I stood in the doorway, for some reason not wanting to enter the darkness held inside that room.

"Luis?"

He didn't answer. There was no sound, except, very faintly, I could hear him breathing.

"Luis?"

When again he didn't answer, I left him there and went up the stairs to bed. Mum stood in the doorway of her room, hands clasped at her breast.

"Is he all right?"

"It was just a bad dream."

"He . . . " Mum hesitated, holding my gaze. "He's been acting odd, Siobhan, ever since he got back. You've noticed it too. I know you have."

"Go back to bed, Mum. He'll be up in a minute."

As I climbed back into bed, I realized Mum was right. Since his return from Spain, Luis's behavior had become increasingly strange. He would sit in the living room for hours staring in silence at the TV without switching it on. Or Mum and I would return from a walk to find him at the kitchen table, absorbed with drawing intricate patterns of leaves on his hands and fingers, sometimes up his forearms as far as his elbow.

When we asked what he was doing, he'd look baffled and stare at his hands as if someone else had done those drawings without him realizing.

It was clear something was wrong. Very wrong. I just hadn't wanted to acknowledge it.

Climbing out of bed again, I crept back downstairs. Standing in the living room doorway, I said into the dark: "Luis, I want to help you. Tell me how I can help you."

When there was no answer, I reached around the doorframe and found the light switch. But Luis wasn't in the room. I found him cross-legged on the floor of the downstairs toilet, with copies of Theodore Munroe's photographs—the ones that had given me such a chill—spread out on the tiles. Before he could stop me, I swept them all up in my hands and screwed them into a ball. Clambering to his feet, Luis followed me into the kitchen where I pushed the ball of paper deep into the bin.

"Siobhan—what the hell?"

"You told me we were going to forget all that," I said, rounding on him. My heart was beating fast, and anger coursed through me. I'm not sure why I was so furious. Perhaps I was afraid. Seeing those pictures again, however briefly, had brought back all the unease I'd felt when I first looked at them. "You said we were going to put it behind us. Why on earth did you get those pictures out again? What do you want to keep looking at them for?"

"I'm trying," Luis said, lowering his voice, "to understand what happened out there. I want to be certain I didn't just imagine it all. Maybe then . . . "

"Did you see something?" I looked closely at him. "Did you

see what killed them? The others? Did you?"

His eyes grew wide. He shook his head.

"And what do you think it was? You know, right? You know something."

"The..." His voice became almost inaudible. "The duende."

"Duende? What the hell are duende?"

"Goblins. Elves." He threw up his hands. "Something like that. I don't know. Fairies. Little demons."

I couldn't help laughing. "Fairies? For God's sake, Luis."

"It's true, Siobhan. I saw the lights. Balls of light floating a foot off the ground. There was a trail of them leading deeper into the woods. How do you explain that?"

"You must have imagined it."

"No." He shook his head again. "We all saw them."

"Then Munroe dosed your dinner with magic mushrooms."

His brow knit. I could tell by his expression that he hadn't considered this. He drew back.

"You . . . you think that's what could've happened?"

"I don't know. You all paid a lot of money to go on that trek, didn't you? You had to see something, right? To make it worthwhile. He could have spiked you with something to make sure you did. And somehow it all went horribly wrong. But Theodore Munroe was a fraud, Luis. That's what I think." I drew in a deep breath. "I'm going back to bed."

"Siobhan . . ."

"It's late, Luis. I . . ."

As I turned to leave the kitchen, I heard Holly start to cry.

"Great. That's great." I began preparing a bottle with formula milk.

"Do you want me to do it?" Luis said.

"No, you get some sleep. It's fine. I can manage."

By the time I'd fed Holly and got her settled again, Luis was fast asleep in our bed. Instead of climbing in beside him, some compulsion made me go downstairs to the kitchen and retrieve that wad of screwed up paper from the bin. I smoothed each of the pictures out as best I could on the work surface. In one of the pictures there was what looked like a trail of glowing orbs leading into the darkness under a clutch of trees.

Balls of light floating a foot off the ground. We all saw them.

Another picture, if you squinted at it, might have shown a group of small retreating figures. They did not look human—there was something off about their shape, too squat, limbs too long—but it was difficult to say for sure. The picture had been enlarged so that it had become blurred and pixelated.

Still . . .

An icy finger ran down my spine. I felt as if someone watched me through the half open kitchen door. I turned to look. There was nothing. No one. Just the dark hallway.

I returned to the papers laid out on the work surface. I picked up the one that seemed to have figures in it, bringing it closer to my face.

Fairies. Little demons.

Crazy.

I gathered all the pictures together, screwed them up and tossed them back into the bin.

OVER THE WEEKS that followed, Luis began to seem more himself. He'd had the cast on his arm removed weeks earlier, and the wound on his head had healed leaving only a faint scar. He helped with the baby, and began ringing round his contacts in search of work. The only blip in our relationship came when I suggested it might be a bit soon for him to take on another assignment and he told me, "We can't exist forever on our savings and your maternity pay, Siobhan. We need money coming in." I took this as a little barbed attack on my lowly receptionist job, and I remembered how I'd impressed him on our first date by telling him about all the books I'd read, how I loved Dickens and Austen and Lawrence. How I'd even tried to write a few short stories myself. "You're not just some little dentist's receptionist, are you?" he'd said that day, and I'd felt as if someone were truly seeing me for the first time. Now he seemed to be telling me that was all I was, that I couldn't support our family without his help and, true or not, it hurt and so I didn't speak to him for a couple of days. I don't know if he was still having nightmares, but he no longer woke up shouting in the middle of the night.

"You know I think you were right, Siobhan," he said to me one day. "Munroe must have spiked us all with something on that trip. I don't know why I didn't see it sooner. It's the only thing that makes sense."

Seeing the change in him, Mum decided she was surplus to requirements, and went home to Dad. I didn't speak to Luis about his Spanish trip, just as he'd insisted I didn't, but I kept an eye on developments in the news. Two skulls had been found in the hollow of a tree, along with the passports of a Japanese couple who'd been part of Munroe's group, and police were investigating. After two months the search parties, having still not turned up any of the missing, were called off. People on Twitter talked about it being a hoax, something Munroe and Wilder Black, the missing film star, had concocted as a publicity stunt. Attention waned. By September, I began to truly feel that the whole thing was behind us, and we could get on with being a family: Me, Luis, and Holly.

Then one night I was wrenched awake by two sounds. One was Holly crying. The other was a loud banging, which seemed to be coming from downstairs. I sat up, realizing Luis was gone from the bed. I rushed to the box room and picked Holly up out of her cot. She quietened a little as I cradled her in my arms. I went to the top of the stairs and switched on the landing light. The front door stood open and Luis was crouched on the threshold.

"Luis?"

I descended a few stairs, trying to work out what the hell he was doing. He appeared to be hammering big thick nails into the floorboards at the entrance to the house.

I clutched Holly against my chest. "Luis? *Luis?* It's the middle of the night. What in God's name are you doing?"

He turned to look at me, his eyes wild.

"What do you think, Siobhan? I'm protecting us."

"Protecting us? From what?"

"From the duende," he said. "They aren't finished with me yet. They want Holly."

A cold shock went through me when he said that. "Holly? What are you talking about?"

"They want to take Holly as punishment for me trespassing in their wood. For the lack of respect I showed. But don't worry, I won't let it happen."

Luis grabbed a handful of nails from the box and showed them to me in his open palm. They were large, thick nails, just as I'd thought. God knows where he'd got them from.

"These will make a barrier," he said, "so they can't enter the house. It's the iron. They're iron nails. The iron will keep them out. I'll do the back door as well. So they can't cross the threshold."

"Luis, for God's sake, you've probably woken all the neighbors with that banging. Someone's going to call the police. Stop what you're doing and come back to bed. Now!"

"I have to finish this."

"Have you lost your mind? Please! Just stop."

Putting his back to me, he went on hammering nails into the floorboards. I pleaded with him further, begged with him to stop, but he wouldn't. So I carried Holly back to the bedroom, closed the door, sat on the bed, clutched my baby against me and wept. Eventually, the hammering stopped but it soon started again from another place in the house and I knew Luis had moved on to the back door.

"Your daddy's lost his mind," I whispered to Holly, wiping the tears from my cheeks with one hand. She gazed up at me, her face stamped with incomprehension as if she too were wondering what the hell was going on. I thought then that she was the most beautiful thing I'd ever seen, her big brown eyes, lively and intelligent, seeming to read my face, to know everything already without having to understand my words. I remembered how Luis had said *they want Holly,* and I felt sick with fear. "He's completely lost his mind, babe. We're going to have to get him some help."

Eventually the hammering stopped. I waited, but Luis didn't come back to bed.

I fell asleep sitting up with Holly in my arms.

When I woke I lay on my side. There was light behind the curtains. I was alone. The baby was gone. Had Luis put her in the cot during the night? With an acute sense of dread, I got up and rushed into the box room. The cot was empty.

"Luis?"

I ran downstairs. By the front door I noticed the mess Luis had made of the floorboards, and any hope that the night's events had been some horrible nightmare vanished.

"Luis?"

He was in the lounge, wearing only his boxers, with Holly laid out beside him on the sofa. She wore only her nappy. When I saw them I screamed. I didn't know what it was, you see? What he'd done it with. Not at first. Later I realized it was felt-tip pen. Green felt-tip pen. He had drawn leaves and vines all over Holly's body, on her chest and legs and arms, and even on her face and head. He'd done the same to himself, on all the places he could reach.

"Luis—what in god's name . . . !"

I picked up Holly and carried her back upstairs. On the bedside table, I found some wet wipes and began cleaning the ink from her face. I was so angry my hands shook. Luis appeared in the bedroom doorway, looking at me in bemusement.

"Luis, what the hell is wrong with you?" I yelled. "Look . . . look what you did to her."

Holly started to bawl. I held her against me and rocked her.

"Shush. Shush."

Without a word, Luis ducked back into the hall. What next? I wondered. What now? It was then that I realized I had to get out of there. If Luis could draw all over his own child's face, and hammer nails into the floor in the middle of the night, what else might he be capable of? Where would this madness end?

After pulling on some clothes, I dressed Holly, dragged a sports bag out of the wardrobe and began tossing a few things into it. Then I picked up the baby and with her in one arm and the bag in the other I went downstairs. I was in the kitchen, buckling Holly into her car-seat when Luis reappeared through the backdoor. Barefoot, and still in his boxers, he'd been out in the garden. There was mud and leaves stuck to his body, and he'd jammed twigs into his hair and into the waistband of his boxers.

Seeing me, he halted. "Going somewhere?"

Car-seat in one hand, and bag in the other, I walked toward the front door. "We're going to stay with Mum for a while."

"You're leaving me?"

"We're going to get you some help. You're not yourself."

"Don't go. Please."

"I have to. We're not safe here."

"Safe?"

I heard his quick feet behind me. I started to run, but he reached the front door before me and threw himself against it.

"The iron will keep out the duende, Siobhan. I promise. You have to trust me."

"It's not the duende I'm worried about, Luis. It's you. Look what you did to Holly . . . to yourself."

He looked down and seemed shocked to see the mess he'd made of himself. I took advantage of his bafflement to push past him and get the door open.

Our elderly neighbor, Anne, emerged from her house when she saw me buckling Holly's seat into the car.

"Siobhan," she said, "is everything all right? What on earth was all that racket last night? You woke Jerry and me up with all that hammering. At three o'clock in the morning."

"I'm sorry," I said. "We're having a few issues with Luis."

"Issues? What issues?"

"He's not well."

"Not . . . "

She turned on the spot and saw Luis standing in the doorway of our house, a mess of mud and leaves and green felt-tip pen. Letting out a short little scream, she scurried back to her house and slammed the door.

"Siobhan?" Luis called.

"I'm going to get you some help, Luis," I called back as I climbed into the car. "I promise."

I reversed off the drive and turned the car around. Driving away, I saw Luis in the rearview, still standing in the doorway of the house. He looked lost, child-like, and I felt a wash of remorse to be leaving him like that.

But I had Holly to think of.

I looked at her. She watched me, eyes big and round.

IT WAS OUR neighbor, Anne, who called me at my parent's house. I'd been there for three days, ringing around various mental health agencies trying to get some advice on what to do about

Luis. I didn't know if he was having some kind of mental breakdown, if he was suffering from PTSD, or if he'd been spiked with acid or mushrooms during his foray in Spain and it had triggered some kind of psychosis. All I knew was he needed help, that much was clear, but everyone I spoke to told me to take him to see his GP. I had called his GP, of course. That was the first thing I'd done. But the only available appointment was three weeks away, and I knew in my heart Luis couldn't wait that long.

"What sort of healthcare system is this?" I said to Mum, who often stood close by fretting as I spoke on the phone. "What are you supposed to do in an emergency?"

I hadn't spoken to my husband since leaving the house. Every time I tried his mobile number, it went straight to voicemail. I didn't like the idea of him being alone, but I couldn't face going back there either. Not yet. Dad said he would pay him a visit, to check he was okay, but then he hurt his back raking leaves in the garden and was laid up in bed. Mum and I were discussing what to do when the phone rang.

"It's for you," Mum said, holding out the receiver. Her face looked fraught. "It's that busybody neighbor of yours."

"Hello?"

"Siobhan," the voice on the other end said. "Siobhan? Is that you?"

A feeling of dread began to uncoil inside of me. "Yes. Hi, Anne. What's up? Is something wrong?"

"Siobhan, listen. You have to do something about Luis."

"Luis? What . . . what do you mean?"

"Have you two had a fight or something?"

"No. Of course not. I'm just staying with my folks for a few days. Why? What's the matter?"

"He's gone crazy, Siobhan. Banging and shouting at all hours of the day and night. And we've seen him dragging great big tree branches and all sorts into the house. Jerry went round there yesterday to speak to him, but Luis wouldn't answer the door. Jerry said he looked in the window and the front room was in a terrible state. Said it looked like Luis was building some kind of nest in there."

"A . . . nest?"

My hand that was holding the phone started to shake.

"We're close to calling the police. He's been waking us up at all hours. The night before last we heard screaming."

"Screaming?"

"Yes. We don't know what the hell's going on in there. If this goes on I'm sorry to say we'll be forced to . . . Siobhan?"

I felt numb. "Don't worry, Anne. I'm coming back to speak to him, okay?"

"We'll call the police, Siobhan, if this goes on. What choice do we have?"

"No, don't do that. I'll come back. I'll speak to him."

"This can't . . . "

I set the receiver down in its cradle, cutting off Anne's voice.

Mum stood in the kitchen doorway, staring at me in concern. "What? What is it?"

"I have to go check on Luis."

Mum's eyes widened. "Why? What's he doing now?"

"I don't know." I shook my head, covering my face with

my hands. "He's . . . sounds like he's gone mad. Just . . . completely mad. I'll have to go and see."

"You can't go alone," Mum said. "I'll come."

"No. You stay here. I'm leaving Holly with you."

"I can't let you go there alone, Siobhan."

"I'll be fine. He'd never do anything to hurt me."

Mum's eyes widened. She must have picked up on the lack of conviction I too had heard in my voice.

I FELT SICK with dread as I pulled into the driveway of our house. The day was overcast and still. I saw no one as I drove onto the cul-de-sac. All the houses looked grey and silent. To me it seemed as if the noise of the car door closing and my footsteps up the driveway were the only sounds left in the world. There was something terrible about seeing all those two-up two-down houses with their neat little gardens, all that hyper-normality, when I was certain something awful awaited me inside my own home. The quiet and the stillness seemed to me strangely ominous, like an augury of something bad, the kind of thing you remember when you look back. "The day was so calm and quiet," you tell people. "Who could think I was about to . . . ?"

The living room curtains were drawn. I tried to look through the little mottled window in the front door, but saw nothing. My hands trembled as I fit my key into the lock.

The door struck against something as I tried to open it, leaving a space just big enough for me to squeeze through. Struggling to fit, I became aware of a smell from inside: thick and pungent. An earthy smell of rot and decay.

"Luis? Oh my God."

I couldn't believe what I was seeing. Behind the front door, he'd created a kind of archway using logs and tree branches. A secondary entrance. I had to duck down to pass through. I stumbled. The hallway floor was carpeted with dead leaves and clods of earth, some with grass sticking out of them. Tree branches were leaned against the walls. More soil and dead leaves covered the stairs, and he'd threaded twigs and vines through the spindles of the banister.

"*Jesus.* What the . . . ?"

Already, I wanted to weep seeing what he'd done. This was our home. It was Holly's home.

But it was only the beginning. I knew it was. I could only imagine what destruction he'd brought to the rest of the house.

"Luis?" I continued tentatively down the hall, careful where I put my feet.

My breath caught when I looked into the living room. It was unrecognizable. Soil and dead leaves covered every surface. The walls were caked with mud, and a jumble of tree branches and what looked like hacked-apart hedgerow bushes were arranged in front of the window.

The kitchen was in a similar state. Worms wriggled in dirt on the countertop. I looked just long enough to be sure Luis wasn't in there.

I had to stop and take a breath before I started up the stairs. Climbing through all that soil and those piles of leaves, I felt as if I were not ascending but sinking. Sinking down into the earth. When I got to the top, I looked along the hallway. Holly's room was closest, but the door was shut and I daren't open it. I didn't want to believe Luis would cover his baby daughter's bedroom in muck and tree branches and rotting leaves. I made instead for our bedroom. The door stood open. I looked inside.

How to describe what I saw?

Like the rest of the house, Luis had carpeted the room with dirt and leaves. That smell of decay was worst here. It made me pause. Though the curtains were drawn, enough light filtered through for me to see what lay on the bed. I thought of my neighbor, Anne, telling me: *looks like he's building a nest.* It did look like a nest. A huge nest of woven branches and vines and God knows what else. Except this nest was turned over on its side, and had a conical shape so that it looked kind of like a tunnel. A short tunnel.

A tunnel to what?

Luis sat cross-legged on the floor at the foot of the bed. He was naked, but his body was caked in mud. He'd wrapped what looked like ivy around his arms and legs and torso. Somehow, he'd fastened twigs into his hair so that they looked like antlers. He faced forward, staring into the nest or tunnel or whatever that thing was supposed to be that lay on top of our bed.

At the sight of him, I let out a little sob, and at this he turned his head.

"Siobhan."

"Luis . . ." Tears came then. I felt them hot on my cheeks. "What is all this? What're you doing in here?"

"I made a gateway for them," he said, lifting one hand and pointing at the thing on the bed. "They made me do it."

"Who, Luis? Who made you?"

"The duende. They're here."

There was a loud crash from somewhere further along the hall, possibly Holly's room, which startled me so much that I let out a little scream.

Taking a step back, I looked along the hall to Holly's room. The door remained closed. I looked back at Luis.

"Is someone in Holly's room?"

"They want her," Luis said. "They're looking for her. You have to keep her away from them. You have to keep her safe."

"Luis, this is our home. Who's in here? What've you done?"

"I told you," he said.

I retraced my steps back down the hall and paused in front of my daughter's bedroom. I put my ear to the closed door. I heard nothing at first. Then, a kind of thwarted shriek that scared me so much I stumbled backwards to the head of the stairs. Before fully realizing it, I was half-running, half sliding down those stairs. Again, I had that sensation I was sinking, only this time I imagined hands were pushing up through the dirt and leaves covering the stairs and clutching at my feet and ankles, dragging me down. As I tried to escape the house, my sweater caught on that arch Luis had made by the front door, and I yanked on it to free myself, tearing the sweater and bringing half the arch crashing down on top of me. I threw it off and reached for the handle on the front door. It was then that I realized something had a hold of me from behind. I didn't look to see what it was. I couldn't breathe. My mouth was somehow full of soil. It filled my airways. I choked on it. Gagged. Spat. I struggled and thrashed, and somehow managed to break free of whatever held on to me. Throwing open the front door, I ran screaming to the car.

I'd driven a few miles, veering from side to side on the road, before I came to my senses and pulled over. I was sobbing, my whole body shaking. My sweater was torn open at the shoulder, and looking in the rearview mirror, I saw that I had a gash across my left cheekbone that oozed blood down the side of my face. Dirt and saliva was streaked around my mouth and on my chin. My eyes were wide in alarm. A twig had caught in my hair. I pulled it out, frantically rolled down the side window, and threw it out.

I waited, trying to get my breathing under control. In my mind, I ran through what I'd seen in the house, trying to make sense of it. I couldn't.

Over and over in my mind, I heard Luis saying: *You have to keep her away from them, Siobhan. You have to keep her safe.*

WINTER'S ON ITS way. The trees in the garden have shed their remaining leaves. I feel glad. Nature's retreating. Dying off. But it'll return in spring. That's why we have to go.

I knew we'd have to leave my parents' house when I discovered bindweed growing through a crack in the window frame of the room where Holly and I sleep. It had grown under the fence from the garden next door, climbed the drainpipe and pushed its way in.

Dad said I was over-reacting. He sealed the crack, but I knew the bindweed would find another way in.

According to my Google search, Plymouth has less green space than any other city in the UK, apart from London. I'm not ready for London. Maybe one day.

TIM JEFFREYS short fiction has appeared in *Supernatural Tales, The Alchemy Press Book of Horrors 2 & 3, Nightscript 4, Stories We Tell After Midnight 2 & 3, Cosmic Horror Monthly #1, Shadow Plays* from P.S. Publishing, and many other places. His ghost story novella, *Holburn*, was released by Manta Press in 2022. The sequel, *Back from the Black*, came out in 2023. Other work includes the comic horror novella, *Here Comes Mr Herribone!*, and sci-fi novella, *Voids*, co-written with Martin Greaves, and the novel *The False Ones*, due for release in February 2025 from Crossroads Press. www.timjeffreysblogspot.com

MIXED SIGNALS

Michael McKeown Bondhus

Danforth first heard the signal on a cold night in 1985. An ice storm had knocked out the TV aerial, so he was playing with the shortwave radio Chip had left behind. Danforth didn't know anything about shortwave, and, at the time, neither did Chip. "A hobby-in-waiting," Chip had said. "All kinds of crazy shit out there. Spies, police, guerrillas, Soviet propaganda." Danforth understood the appeal of pursuing a good mystery, but he couldn't get past the reality that anything they encountered would have to remain a mystery. There was no way to break coded spy messages that he knew of, no way to see how a police call-up turned out. Danforth preferred mysteries with resolutions. But now, with nothing better to do, he was skimming frequencies and picking up little more than static.

Out the window, white flakes fell close together, nearly obscuring the black of night. Suddenly, a buzz sounded from the midst of the crackle. He paused, hoping it was the prelude to something interesting. A moment later, it repeated. It appeared to be a regular pattern—every four seconds. It was like the sound a kazoo makes, mixed with static.

The buzz sounded a third time, and Danforth saw an industrial light fixture, circular, orange-yellow in color, guarded by a steel cage. He blinked and it was gone. The shortwave buzzed again and the image reappeared. The light crackled then faded, like fire catching a dry leaf.

Was this a hallucination or an act of involuntary imagination, Danforth wondered. Was there a difference?

Buzz.

Again his living room disappeared and he was standing in the industrial light's harsh glare. Then it flickered out and he was back in his living room.

Before it could happen a fourth time, Danforth switched off the radio. He brushed his teeth, undressed, and crawled into bed. He lay there for a few minutes and stared at the ceiling before consciously deciding that whatever had just happened had not, in fact, happened.

The next morning he got up, ate breakfast, and shoveled snow. He went to work and chose not to think about the buzzer.

His resolution lasted throughout the day until the evening,

when, after a dinner of grilled cheese and tomato soup, he found himself making involuntary buzzing noises with his mouth. He positioned his easy chair beside the shortwave and turned it on. Leaning back, he folded his hands on his chest and closed his eyes.

Buzz. Again the industrial lamp made its appearance. He knew he could simply be seeing what he expected to see. He considered making a conscious effort to *not* see the light but quickly dismissed the idea. If you decide not to think of a white bear, you'll think of a white bear, he reasoned.

As if in response to his thoughts, the image changed.

Now, instead of an industrial light fixture, he saw a rusted-out lamppost beside a set of lonely railroad tracks. Like the industrial light, the lamp flickered, crackling like a roach's carapace under a boot. A forlorn, weather-beaten shack that must've been the train station hunched in the darkness. Snow fell quietly on the evergreen forest that grew on either side of the tracks. Black clouds roiled in a starless, purple sky.

The scene vanished before Danforth could process it fully. He waited expectantly for the next buzz to return him to the forested train station.

He never heard it. Instead, he *felt* it. The buzz crackled through his head, like lizards running across his scalp. His hands gripped the arms of the chair as his muscles twitched, more out of surprise than anything else. Four seconds later, the sensation repeated. He jumped to his feet and switched off the radio. He stood for a long time, breathing heavily.

He calmed himself with a cup of lavender tea. The warm, purple taste carried him through the rest of his bedtime routine.

Once under the covers, he forced himself to stop thinking about the winter train station and the buzzing sensation he'd felt in his scalp. He was normally good at controlling his thoughts. Chip used to call him "Obi-Wan" because of his imperturbable sense of equilibrium. Maybe he really was attuned to the Force and that was why he was having visions whenever the signal buzzed . . . a sort of Pavlovian Jedi.

But the signal hadn't buzzed the last two times, had it? He hadn't actually *heard* the last two buzzes. He had just felt them. He was certain of it.

What he wasn't certain of was whether he had heard a buzz when the scene by the winter train tracks had manifested. He thought he had, but he couldn't be sure. Recalling the scene now, it appeared to him fuzzy, granulated. There had been something static-like about the snow. The tracks and the train station were discernible but blurry. The forest surrounding the station had seemed like one dark mass rather than a dense arrangement of individual trees. Had the sound caused his mind to *generate* the image or had his mind translated the sound *into* an image? He considered going back to the living room and listening again but instead forced himself to stay in bed. It took awhile, but he finally managed to sleep.

The next day, Danforth went rooting through what was left of Chip's things until he found a stack of *Waveforms*, the radio enthusiast magazine Chip had subscribed to and seldom read. There was a year's worth of issues, many of them untouched. Typical. Not like Danforth, who made it a point to read *TIME* every Saturday morning before lunch and discard it in the evening's trash.

"You're just so... agonizingly... *dependable*," Chip had said.

"One of us has to be," Danforth had shot back.

"Don't treat me like I'm a loser!"

"Jesus Christ," Danforth had sighed. "You could be anything you want, but you just don't try." He hated sounding like his dad, but he hadn't known what else to say.

"What makes you think I don't want more? Just because I'm not interested in chasing some shitty office job . . ."

Danforth had tried to get Chip to elaborate. What did he want? To be a musician? A movie star? A corporate shark? Chip never gave a clear answer, claiming that Danforth wouldn't get it—a downright adolescent response.

A few months later, the two separated. Danforth was tired of paying Chip's way. Chip claimed that Danforth was "holding him back." Danforth had no idea what he could possibly be holding Chip back from, nor did he care. Their good-bye was stiff and polite.

Danforth flipped through the pristine magazines, uncertain what he was looking for. An exposé on strange transmissions? He noticed there was a regular "letters from readers" section and decided to be proactive. He sat at his desk and wrote a detailed description of the buzzing station. He provided the frequency and the town he lived in (he wasn't sure if the latter was important). He ended with a request for whatever information the magazine or its readers might have on the signal.

Six weeks passed. Danforth lived his routine—6am jog, 7am breakfast, work from 8 to 5, 90 minutes of reading, dinner, the evening news, one hour of listening to the buzz, and in bed at 9:30. Night after night, the signal buzzed along and Danforth saw either industrial lights crackling warmly in the forlorn darkness of a vacant factory or a rusted lamppost glowing beside a snowy train station. Sometimes he experienced the scalp tingling again. Every time he settled in to listen, he reminded himself to note whether the images *accompanied* the buzz or *replaced* it. Every time he emerged from his trance he was just as uncertain as ever. He could recall buzzes and he could recall images but he was never sure if any of them had occurred simultaneously.

When the next issue of *Waveforms* arrived (he had also written a check for nine bucks to cover another year's subscription), Danforth was disappointed to see that they had not printed his query. His disappointment evaporated the next day, however, when he received a letter from *Waveforms* editorial staff informing him that his was not the first inquiry they had received re: "that frequency with the buzz." Shortwave hobbyists interested in mysterious transmissions had formed a correspondence club, and the editor had passed Danforth's letter on to them.

Inwardly, Danforth commended the editor's initiative. He was even more pleasantly surprised when the very next day he received the aforementioned club's most recent newsletter along with a brief note from one of the members, welcoming him. The newsletter was nothing fancy—a folded broadside which Danforth suspected had been sneakily xeroxed on an office copy machine. In the margin was a generic sketch of a radio tower with jagged energy lines shooting out of it. The name of the newsletter was "The Buzzer."

Danforth perused it with interest. It mostly contained reports of listeners' experiences with the so-called Buzzer. A man from Kailua wrote that he always kept The Buzzer on while he was sleeping because it made him dream about floating through the deepest, emptiest regions of space. A woman from Akron claimed that she had felt compelled to listen to it every night for the past eight years. Her listening sessions had started at 15 minutes and gradually grown to three hours. Now she found it impossible to sleep if she didn't listen to the signal before bed. A man in Tallahassee wrote that his sense of taste had become permanently altered after a few months of listening to The Buzzer. It was subtle but noticeable—a slight metallic underflavor to everything. Danforth thought about the images of the industrial light and the snowy depot, the buzzing crawl across his scalp.

Speculations about the nature of the signal ran wild. Some thought it came from aliens. Some thought it was a secret Soviet asset. Others believed it was a cryptid trapped in ice and calling for help. As for its source, one of the group members had triangulated the signal and determined that it was coming from northern Greenland. He had published the coordinates, clearly hoping some club member would take a jaunt above the Arctic Circle.

That evening, Danforth tuned into the signal again. This time, there were no visions or tactile sensations. The familiar buzz sounded at four-second intervals, but Danforth's consciousness remained squarely in his living room. Had his investigations into the signal somehow triggered the more rational part of his brain, thereby short-circuiting the hallucinations? A sense of loss, startling in its intensity, overwhelmed him.

Danforth was about to switch the radio off when he heard a sharp, squealing crackle, as if a microphone had been pushed too close to a speaker. Someone inhaled loudly through their nose and then cleared their throat. There was another loud crackling, and then a low voice mumbled something indiscernible. Danforth turned the volume up and leaned close to the speaker.

The words were garbled and intercut with static. Danforth grabbed a pen and began to jot down his best approximations of the broken, guttural sounds.

Hrum.

Ulch.

Karg.

Hroll.

Fung.

As he wrote, he realized that each monosyllable was just that—a complete unit of sound and, presumably, meaning. They were not fragments of longer words. Yet they didn't sound like any language he knew. The only familiar thing about the words was the voice they were uttered in.

"Chip?"

He felt foolish whispering his ex-lover's name into the speaker of a one-way radio.

The radio responded.

"Here."

There was a four second pause, then he heard it again.

"Here."

It was definitely Chip's voice.

"Here."

"Chip!" he yelled.

"Here."

"Chip!"

Buzz.

Danforth stared at the radio.

Buzz.

He collapsed into his chair. A noise emerged from his throat that was part gasp and part sob.

Buzz.

He heard it in his right arm. He looked down and saw—just for a moment—a ripple or a crease in the forearm. It was there, then it was gone. He slapped at the spot and then cursed as the sound boomed in his head.

"Chip!" He didn't know why he was saying his name again. "Chip!" The word ran down his chin and got tangled in his beard. He could feel it pulling hair away from his face.

Danforth ran to the kitchen. His steps echoed in his left elbow. He threw open the cabinet, took out a glass, and filled it in the sink. The sound of running water tickled his left knee. He raised the glass to his lips and paused. How would water taste? Where would he taste it? The thought terrified him.

He stared at the half-full glass in his hand. If he drank, would he smell the water instead of tasting it? Water didn't have a smell, but it didn't exactly have a taste either.

Trying not to think anymore about it, he downed the tap water in one gulp. To his immense relief, he felt the predictable sensation of cold, quenching nothingness fill his mouth and slide down his throat. He opened his mouth to speak. He almost said "Chip" but stopped himself.

"Hello," he said lamely to the empty kitchen. The sound left his mouth and settled in his ears. His arms, knees, and elbows remained sensationless.

Buzz.

He nearly dropped the glass into the sink before realizing he'd left the damn radio on. He stormed into the living room, more angry than afraid, and switched it off. Either the signal was making him crazy or some entity was using it as a conduit to antagonize him. He didn't really believe the second possibility, but the first was bothersome enough. He would get rid of the damn thing in the morning.

Night came and went. Danforth slept better than he'd expected to. He woke up with a plan. Jog, eat breakfast, pack up the shortwave, and drop it off at the Goodwill before work. It was an expensive piece of equipment, but at least he could get a tax write-off. He was *certain* that he'd imagined hearing things with his arm. He was also certain that Chip couldn't be in Greenland. He could sooner imagine Reagan staffing a radio station at the North Pole. It had to have been someone else. Romantic images of KGB agents communicating in coded monosyllables filled his head.

He drove to the Goodwill and saw, to his dismay, that the parking lot was flooded with cars. He remembered it was Tuesday, when all blue ticketed items were on sale. It always attracted swarms of old folks. He turned around and drove to the office. He would drop the radio off that evening.

Five o'clock rolled around. He was preparing to head for the Goodwill when a few coworkers asked him if he wanted to join them for happy hour. He didn't get out often, and company seemed like a good way to bring him fully back to reality after spending the previous evening in the Twilight Zone. By the time he left the bar, the donation center was closed. Tomorrow, then. When he got home, he left the radio in the car. No point carrying it in just to carry it back out.

The next morning Danforth woke up with a headache. It reminded him of the time when he'd discovered he didn't have any coffee left for breakfast. It was a small but noticeable discomfort, a dull ache clustered behind his eyes. After a few moments of rubbing his forehead, he decided to skip the morning jog and instead go into work early. That way he could drop off the radio too and be done with it.

It was in the car where Danforth had left it the night before, stashed beneath an old blanket. He drove to the Goodwill and was surprised to see it closed. Then he remembered they didn't open until eight. He went to work and vowed to return to the donation center that evening, hell or high water.

As the day progressed, his headache lingered. The pressure behind his eyes prevented him from looking at the spreadsheets' tiny print for more than a few minutes at a time. Every now and then he'd hear or feel a buzz and he'd jerk his head up and look around, like a rabbit peering out of its burrow. The disturbance was always distinct enough to seem real, yet brief enough to be chalked up to imagination. Unlike the long, pronounced buzzes he heard on the shortwave, these were short and clipped. It felt like someone was making fun of him, lightly poking the part of his brain where hallucinations slept.

At the end of the day, he drove straight home. He took the shortwave out of the car, brought it back to the living room, plugged it in, and turned it on.

Buzz.

The tension behind his eyes evaporated.

Buzz.

He opened his eyes and saw it—a swarm of vibrating black dots.

Buzz.

He felt them on his tongue. They tasted like pepper.

Here.

Chip's voice again.

Here.

HE WASN'T SURPRISED when he saw the train station from his vision. It meant he was close. The guide had taken him as far as the nearest village, but he would need to find his own way to the transmission. In addition to the coordinates, he had a compass, a sextant, an insulated jacket, and a snowmobile.

He'd told himself it was about love and desire, a bizarre radio signal calling him to rekindle a relationship with the man he'd spent five fickle years with. It made no sense, but "there are more things in heaven and earth, etc." He'd never really believed that, of course, but it had been enough to get him onto the plane. The truth was, quite simply, that nothing could do to his body what the signal did to it. Now his senses had senses. His skin could hear and see. His ears could taste language and smell music. The black dots had just been the beginning. The ugly barcalounger he reclined in every night to listen to the signal filled his mouth with a rich, creamy, cola taste. When his bare toes ran through the shag carpeting, he smelled the fresh heat of the desert (he had never been to a desert, but he intuitively knew this was what a desert smelled like). The sound of cars swishing through rain was familiar fingers touching his cheek. The signal had awakened everything. He had to find its source. And if Chip really was there, well, maybe they'd be lovers again. Even though he wasn't doing this for Chip, the knowledge that he was somehow part of it made the whole venture feel safer . . . and perhaps even vaguely sane.

The closer Danforth got to the source, the less necessary the sextant and compass became. He felt the pulse and call of the signal on his skin. It filled his nose with the smell of wet metal. Drifting above him he thought he could see jagged waveforms glowing like neon eye floaters. Was this what it was like to be an animal tracking its prey? He followed his senses from the derelict train station, through evergreen forests, over drifting hills of snow. Icy howls tore through his coat as if it were a rain slicker. As he drew closer to the source of the signal, his senses continued to shift. He smelled the wind and heard the falling snow. His clothes tasted like a flavorless warmth which reminded him of eating hot soup with a head cold. The roar of the snow speeder smelled like pine mixed with coconut. Even the purple sky resonated with the crystalline music of the universe.

He came to the source just as the sun was coming up (it reminded him of trombones). He hadn't known what to expect. A starry abyss? A UFO? But the signal was coming from an unremarkable radio tower mounted atop a listening station. No fence surrounded it, no padlock secured the door. He parked his snowmobile and went inside.

The vestibule was lit by a familiar light fixture—circular,

orange-yellow in color, protected by a steel cage. He heard the light singing in his organs, felt its tasteless flicker and crackle on his tongue. His skin heard the stale air as countless small ears blossomed across its surface, puckering his arms like sores. Tiny, yellowed eyes joined the ears, painlessly cracking open his flesh. He was past the point of feeling terror or wonder. The buzz surrounded him like a warm, wet flap of cartilage as he stumbled down the clanking, metal hallway to what he assumed was the entrance to the control room and the epicenter of the signal.

The instant Danforth entered the room, he felt Chip's gaze, heard his scent. His ex-lover's body was invisible and everywhere. He was walking through the skin, muscle, and hair that he had once known intimately. Every air molecule brushed against him like a naked body. The only visible objects in the room were a desk and chair, a microphone which sat on the desk, and a black box that sat by the microphone, emitting the familiar buzz. The box was covered in gray dust. It looked like cardboard, flimsy. Danforth approached it, each step another push through Chip's immaterial body.

He opened the lid.

Chip's presence was drowned out immediately. Danforth gripped the back of the chair to keep from falling. Countless other energies crowded around him. Some were men, some were women, some were both or neither. The eyes and ears rippling across his flesh tensed at the onslaught of sensation. He heard them all, smelled them all, tasted them all. Every single energy hit him with its unique vibration, which then broke down and merged with its neighboring vibrations to form something entirely new.

Danforth felt himself being dragged away, though what exactly was being dragged was unclear. It was as though his body no longer existed; or if it did, it existed solely as a repository for sensory input, a beaker into which a mad scientist had poured every imaginable chemical stimulus. Every knowable sensation—good and bad, familiar and unfamiliar, earthly and extra-dimensional—inundated him like a sonic wave. He saw, tasted, smelled, heard, and felt everything at once. Then the sensations switched channels and he tasted everything he'd just seen, saw everything he'd just heard, and on and on until new sensations that had no correspondence with any of the five human senses swept him even further away. He realized that the spirit—for that was what he was now—possessed an unfathomably large number of senses, and that those senses were constantly multiplying into the infinite void, and that he, Danforth, was, like Chip, finally realizing his full potential.

MICHAEL MCKEOWN BONDHUS (he/him; formerly Charlie) is an Irish-American writer. His books include *Divining Bones* (Sundress, 2018) and *All the Heat We Could Carry* (Main Street Rag, 2013), winner of the Thom Gunn Award. His work's appeared in *Poetry*, *Poetry Ireland Review*, *Hotel Amerika*, *Court Green*, *Hayden's Ferry Review*, *diode*, and *Copper Nickel*. He's received fellowships from the Virginia Center for Creative Arts, the Sundress Academy for the Arts, the Tyrone Guthrie Center (Ireland), and the Hawthornden Castle International Retreat for Writers (UK). He teaches at Raritan Valley Community College and lives in Jersey City, NJ. More at: www.michaelbondhus.com. Instagram: BondhusPoetry

CORPSE MEDICINE

Kathryn Reilly

The pharaoh lay in repose, stately, surrounded by those who would accompany him into the afterlife. Priests gathered, hands full, each carrying an essential element to preserve their former ruler's mortal vessel. Sharp, sacred knives severed abdominal flesh and muscle, peeling back the layers slowly along the incision until hands saturated in blessings entered, removing and jarring each organ. The brain-hook slowly ascended the nose until sharp force jabbed it into the brain. For long minutes, the brain snaked out of the nose, slithering into a wet, glistening pile beside the neck until only an empty cavity remained. Fingers carefully mixed resins and spices, rubbing them into every inch, every pore, before reverently adding salt to draw remaining moisture out. Covering the body completely in salts, the priests left, marking the days to total desiccation.

Several weeks later they returned, burnt herbs blessing the room as they organized new oiled herbs and resins. Removing the salts, they began to massage the skin, reviving it to a more human elasticity. Finally the priests wrapped the prepared body in linens, coating them in resins and spices as well. His journey in the living world complete, the priests closed the sarcophagus and then the chamber's door ensuring his afterlife would never be disturbed.

GROANING, THE ANCIENT door dislodged under the weight of the graverobbers' shoulders. Dust percolated the air, pulled towards nostrils with every labored inhale determined to lodge itself into nasal passages daring to disturb the body within the tomb. It did, coating every internal inch with the taste of decayed, stale time. Their candles' dull flickers encouraged the darkness to seep into their skin; the men unconsciously swiped arms and faces repeatedly trying to dislodge the dark, but it rooted into their epidermis and sat, test-driving the first living beings in the bowels of the burial structure in centuries. Their wrongness in this place settled like a miasma, joining the history of previous transgressions. Curses lived well beyond those that uttered them, but money motivated men beyond their fear.

So the men descended into yet another labyrinth, seeking bodies whose bones still boasted skin.

Hours into navigating the darkness, men of a more modern

age wound through the bowels of the burial tomb. Eventually they stumbled upon the room they sought, hands scraped and trailing blood along uneven floors and walls. Several smaller sarcophagi surrounded the center one. With grim smiles, the men began to tear apart the smaller domiciles, placing the mummies in a pile on two blankets. Sweat soaking through thin linen shirts, they turned towards the pharaoh's and heaved, working together. Moments later the sarcophagus top sighed, whispering of betrayal and soon lay askew; the body within, wrapped in time-befouled linen, existed once again in the world of the living. The tallest robber leaned in and patted the body down searching for hard ridges, hopeful to find amulets or other valuables priests had wrapped within the layers to protect the dead in their journey to the afterlife. His partners set about crowbarring any removable items from the top, prying out jewels or other bounty they might sell. But the bodies themselves often protected ankhs and more jewels, or inscribed scrolls. Finding something near the breastbone, the tallest man pressed the desiccated body until mummified skin slunk under his fingernails. Deft fingers wormed the treasure out between the layers, until its gold-sealed edges glowed softly in the candle's light. A gilded heart scarab weighed heavy upon his hand. Europeans paying for the bodies didn't deserve the treasures it carried. He pocketed his find and moved to help exhume the body. Working quickly, the robbers wrapped the final body in a worn, woven blanket and took everything else of value they could carry. Navigating the narrow passageways, they carried the dead towards the living, towards one final desecration.

THE PROCURER ARRIVED under cover of darkness, standing back

from the throng of apothecaries and nobles and peasants standing on the docks, hoping to offer enough to secure the glut of body parts arriving monthly. This arrival's captain, the Charon of mummies, ferried Egypt's long dead into a European afterlife to be consumed in all manner of ways. Most body parts arrived severed from themselves, in barrels or bags, in heaps climbing the cabin's walls. But the procurer paid well for whole mummies, and the French Charon always had a few safely stowed away. Apothecaries and surgeons paid well for the largest bits, and bidding wars erupted for the remaining fingers and femurs. Employed exclusively by the King, the Procurer arrived last and left quickest, his carriage the last comfort the dead would know. This would be the 57th mummified corpse he'd acquired for the King; the linen-wrapped dead would soon be joining the others.

But two mummies rested in his carriage during the twilight journey, for the King's son had begun acquiring his own supply, for himself and for his loyal followers. For what better way to reward loyalty than ingesting the dead?

As he drove away, a priest arrived, bearing a cross to bless the ship bow to stern. The captain paid him with a foot, which the Procurer knew would be pulverized and whirled with wine for the Court's Sunday mass.

SAFELY STOWING THE prince's secret away, the Procurer followed the King's orders to leave the mummy on the altar of his private chapel before moving it into the castle's torch-lit labyrinths. A priest arrived with a cross and holy book, and proceeded to unwind the linen.

"Rather like gargoyles, aren't they? Dark, stone-gray skin pulling tight against the bones. Ugly. Each one uglier than the last, I'd say. But gargoyles are ugly to scare away something uglier, so our Lord is wise in all things."

The Procurer shrugged, waiting. Payment wouldn't change hands until the mummy lay safely within access of the tools that would dismember it, piece by piece, saws sliding through bones before hammers pulverized them, so pestles could finally alter them into a more pleasing appearance. After all, as all the living know—the eyes consume all sustenance first.

"Gargoyles, yes. Gargoyles of faithful bodies, working to keep the devil's ailments at bay." Humming a hymn, the priest worked quickly, making the sign of the cross over the entire body, anointing the head, and softly reading several passages before rewrapping the corpse and nodding to its bringer.

Carefully, while those within the castle slept, the Procurer made his way to the holding pen and laid the latest arrival on a stack of others.

THE KING BELIEVED what his father had believed and his grandfather before him. Naturally, what the king believed, his people believed. And so when the Second Estate saw the King designate an ever-present pouch about his ordained person for a mixture of mummia and rhubarb, they too sought out the best apothecaries they could afford for mummia of their own. Lately, the King had taken to snorting the mixture to alleviate congestion, and the dark gray dust seemed ever present about his nostrils. The nobility in the innermost circle vying for favor knew they had earned it upon being invited to watch the apothecary work the corpse, chisel in hand, removing small parts to make the mummia fresh for their consumption. Set upon a large stone slab deep within the castle's many unnamed rooms, the mummy lay, amputated, parts siphoned off to ensure the King's health. While local authorities executed witches throughout France for consorting with the Devil, the nobility consumed the pagan dead.

"This, here," the apothecary rasped, pushing ample sleeves back and placing his chisel at the second finger's base on the right hand, "will do well to address your professed intestinal woes. Come closer, lords, and breathe deeply of the body." Bending close, they followed his example, wafting the air towards their noses.

"Quite fragrant that, not at all like the heretical Protestant bodies rotting everywhere. Why not just sprinkle the powder on food? Why must you add it to wine?"

"The body is bitter, itself; its power lies not simply in the spirit trapped within the flesh of a ruler but in the oils rubbed into it. Even now, Ambroise Paré, the famous surgeon in the King's armies uses mummia to treat our soldiers' grievous wounds. If such concoctions can stave off rot by topical application, imagine what they will do for you internally. Healers of old discovered some medicine that, sadly, does not grow in our soils. But our coin brings it to our shores." Taking the hammer, he drove the metal through the skin and bone several times before a crack sounded and the joint separated, similar to live bodies on the rack. Placing the finger on a separate space, he covered the finger with fine cloth and took a hammer to it several times, breaking it into smaller pieces. The sound of the shattering hung haunting the air moments after the hammer waited its next strike.

The first lord turned towards the second, voice low, "It's rather nice, isn't it, the absence of blood? We're to benefit without any mess. Quite nice, isn't it? Bodies without blood?" His companion nodded, watching with rapt attention as the decimation continued. With each blow, the lumps beneath the linen fractured, and the smaller lumps became bug-sized until the linen nearly lay flat. Then, folding the linen, the apothecary brushed the shards off the table's edge into a waiting mortar. Minutes passed as the two noblemen waited, feet beginning to tap, communicating what they dare not say aloud: watching the man grind down the finger, pestle grating their ears as well as the bones, was not an engaging use of their time. Practiced hands circled, forcing the remains into a fine, gray power. Measuring the powder into two separate piles, the learned man then asked, "The wine?"

"Yes, right here," the first nobleman replied, handing a local, uncorked vintage over.

The mummia disappeared in the crimson liquid, swirling down, bonding completely. "Best to have one glass before eating and one glass after."

"And when I need more?"

"Curry the King's favor," the apothecary's hunched form advised. "This room always houses a mummy, but who stands in its presence and imbibes its healing powers, that comes from his majesty's grace. Or perhaps curry the King's issue; he's assured that his line will be well supplied throughout their lives. More mummies arrive monthly, nearly as many as nobles at court, their destiny at my discretion. Alternatively, you could try your luck at the docks; shipments of body parts arrive quite regularly—rarely whole mummies, mind, but parts. You may happen upon a whole leg on a good day, but dozens upon dozens of hands and feet are certain. Pay for a part and pay a good man of the art to prepare it for you."

The second man stepped forward, eager for his share.

"And you, what ailments does your body suffer from?"

"Pains of the head, long ones."

"Yes, yes. You've brought wine as well?"

"Yes, here."

The King's trusted man reached for the bottle, gnarled, calloused hand wrapping over the soft one to steady the bottle. Carefully, he added most of the mummia, then corked the bottle. "Drink several small sips a day, and for prolonged occurrences place a pinch under the tongue," he advised, placing the remaining powder in a small envelope. He turned, walking several steps to a chest. Opening it, he rummaged in the gray darkness until withdrawing an ornate box and removing the lid, took an oyster-sized bone shard from it. "This is mummia skull. Excellent in addressing concerns of the head. Place it in a bottle of spirits and allow it to leech for no less than three weeks. Then, add a bit of the spirit to your wine for added benefit. Always keep it covered by the spirit."

Acknowledging this wisdom with a nod and a bow, the second nobleman accepted his mummia and stepped back.

The King's generous gifts in hand, the noblemen left the darkened room and returned to the Court.

LATER THAT EVENING, the King welcomed his court to view newly complete paintings, all created with mummy brown.

"Not only does mummia soothe the body, but it also soothes the eyes," the monarch praised. The well-dressed ladies and men praised each painting made from people.

ACROSS EUROPE, THE living rubbed salves of the dead into wounds to staunch blood flow, drunk tinctures long steeped in bones or leathery skins, inserted oils speckled with mummified remains or ingested bones and skin pestaled into powders to grace wines or eyes or tongues. All at court clamored for tinctures or powders of the dead, and so did their lovers. Mistresses, believing mummia could quicken life in their womb, applied it before powerful lovers descended upon their beds. Friends shared the dead among themselves, and friends with means sent servants to the docks seeking to collect an eternal supply.

The problem that arose, of course, was of supply. So the men from the sands as well as the men from civilized societies began to make their own mummies fresh from corpses or from those that soon would be despite their violent protestations. Those with coin paid well to enjoy their health and procure corpse medicine for the health of their descendants.

By day, **KATHRYN REILLY** helps students investigate words' power; by night, she resurrects goddesses and ghosts, spinning new speculative tales. Sometimes she even tells the truth. Enjoy poetry in *Shadow Atlas, A Flight of Dragons, Last Girls Club* and new fiction in *Seaside Gothic, Bikes, the Universe, and Everything, Beneath the Yellow Lights,* and *Fish Gather to Listen.* Her rescue mutts hear all the stories first. When she's not working or writing, you can find her rewilding suburban spaces. Follow at @Katecanwrite or visit katecanwrite.com

UNDONE

Warren Benedetto

I'm running. I don't know why.

I hate running. I always have. I used to run because Adelaide ran, and I loved her. She'd wake me at 5 A.M., already fully dressed in her spandex running shorts and sports bra, ready to run to the park, or around the track, or along Lakeshore Drive, or anywhere, really. It didn't matter to her. She just wanted to get up and out, to start her day with some activity to get her heart beating and her blood flowing. I'd remind her of sex's well-documented cardiovascular benefits—along with the additional advantage of not needing to get out of bed to do it—but Adelaide would insist that, no, running was a much better way to kickstart the day.

Despite a near pathological desire to go back to sleep, I would resist the urge to argue with her. Mainly because I loved her, but also because, goddamn, she looked cute in that ponytail she wore when going out for a jog. Instead, I'd roll out of bed and flop to the floor like a rag doll, making jokes about how I have no bones, how I couldn't possibly be expected to run in this condition: boneless, limp-limbed and noodle-legged, barely even human, basically just a pile of cold udon noodles in boxer briefs and an old Motley Crüe T-shirt. "Noodles can't run," I'd say. "Noodles are tired. Noodles need sleep."

Adelaide would poke me in the ribs with her lime green toenails, jabbing my flabby belly and saying, "Get up, Noodles," until I gave in and trudged into the bathroom to brush my teeth and smear on some deodorant. Then I'd slip on my old basketball shorts and a sleeveless T-shirt, lace up the Nikes she bought me from Foot Locker, and follow her out the front door, watching her ponytail bounce as she jogged down the front steps and took off down the street ahead of me.

Adelaide is gone now. I'm not sure how I know that—I'm not even sure what it means. What is "gone?" Not here right now? Not coming back?

Dead?

I used to joke to Adelaide that the only time a person should run is if they're chasing something or being chased. So, as my feet continue pounding on the pavement, I wonder: which is it now?

There's nothing ahead of me but the two lanes of Main

Street, with its coffee houses, antique shops, and local lunch spots. The yellow lines in the center of the road are freshly painted thanks to the fundraising efforts of the Main Street Restoration Committee. The quaint tree-lined street has a slight uphill grade, which makes running up it even more horrible. It's probably only a one-degree slope, but from the way my calves are burning and my thighs are trembling, it feels like I'm running straight up the side of a building.

As I pass under the traffic signal at the intersection of Main Street and Central Avenue, I notice the light flashing red. But it's not a steady flash like I sometimes see when the signal is under maintenance. It's an irregular flicker, like there's some sort of glitch, some kind of electrical interference. The illuminated sign outside the Corner Pharmacy is flickering with a matching cadence—as are the lights inside the store—which makes me wonder if the entire power grid is on the fritz.

A stiff wind buffets my face, causing me to gasp for breath. My lungs seem to have too much air and not enough air at the same time. The breeze carries the smell of smoke and a fine gray powder that I first mistake for snow before remembering that it's only September. No, it's not snow drifting down on me—it's ash.

Sweat drips into my eyes. It burns like acid, and when I try to wipe it away, the cuff of my shirtsleeve is stained with a damp black smear. I look down at my body and am surprised to see I'm wearing a long-sleeved dress shirt and gray cotton slacks. My shoes are wrong, too—I can feel them rubbing the flesh from the sides of my toes and the backs of my heels. They're my work shoes: black leather, skinny laces, stiff soles.

Definitely not running shoes. It's as if I just stood up at my desk at Allstate Insurance and decided to go for a jog. But why would I do that? I'm not with Adelaide. I'm not chasing anything. That leaves only one other explanation for why I'm running.

I'm being chased.

I try to concentrate, to hear beyond the sound of my own pounding feet and labored breathing, to listen for footfalls behind me. I try to imagine who—or what?—might be chasing me. I think I hear a muffled galloping accompanied by a sharp clicking, the sound of soft feet with long claws. Is it a bear? There are bears in this part of the state; I know that for sure. But it doesn't make sense that a bear would be chasing me down Main Street. Even if it was, I would never be able to outrun it, especially not with how out of shape I've gotten since Adelaide left.

A sharp pain explodes in my chest. *She left.* That's what "gone" means. Adelaide is gone because she left. Not to swing by the Foodmart for milk, not to jaunt down to Target to pick up a new sports bra, not to rendezvous with her girlfriends at Tricky Dick's for happy hour. No. She left because she didn't love me anymore, because our relationship had run its natural course, and it was just time to move on, babe, that's all.

It wasn't a surprise. I knew it was coming from the first time I awoke to find her in the shower, her running clothes on the bathroom floor, her hair already lathered with shampoo, the lone hair tie from her ponytail forming a damp black circle on the bathroom counter. She didn't wake me to go for a run—she let me sleep in. And I knew, right from that moment, that I had lost her. Three months later, she was gone.

I should stop running, I think. Just stop and let whatever is chasing me catch me. What difference does it make if I live or die, now that Adelaide is gone? Wouldn't it be better to just lie down in the middle of the road and let the thing behind me rip my throat out? But I can't stop. I want to—I really do—but I can't. It's as if I've lost all free will, as if I'm being driven to run despite my best efforts to give up. My legs and arms churn relentlessly, endlessly—they're entirely out of my control. I'm merely a passenger in an autonomous vessel, a passive observer of my own imminent destruction.

I'm going to run until I die.

The realization comes naturally, as matter-of-fact as if I looked out the window to check the weather and saw that it was raining. The thought brings focus, a sense of heightened awareness of my surroundings, and I realize that the footfalls behind me are not that of a bear at all. It's not the clicking of claws on pavement that I hear; it's the footfalls of an army, feet hitting the ground in perfect synchronization, the sound of a military parade in North Korea, not a single step out of time.

A glimpse of movement out of the corner of my eye causes me to turn my head to my left, and I see that someone is running beside me. It's Elise Watson, the third-grade teacher from Deerfield Elementary School. Her slate-gray hair is pulled back in a loose braid that bounces against her neck as she runs. Mascara-blackened tears stream down her cheeks. She has lost weight since her husband died earlier this year; she looks like a half-deflated version of herself. Dark streaks of perspiration stain her rose-colored blouse and floral print leggings. Like me, she's not dressed for a run either—she's dressed for the classroom, for teaching long division to nine-year-olds. And yet there she is, running in stride next to me.

The sight of Elise makes me wonder who else is around me. I look over my right shoulder, then my left. There's Barton Turnbow, the assistant manager of the Foodmart on Eighth Street. And Marie Sempler, the seamstress from the boutique where my mother used to buy her dresses when I was a kid. And Timmy Paine, the star point guard of the Deerfield Elementary boy's basketball team. There are men and women, boys and girls, young and old, all running in perfect lockstep as far back as I can see down Main Street. They look like a mass of marathon runners who all decided to run in street clothes. Mr. Lindenbaum is even running in his bathrobe.

At first, I think that everyone in Deerfield must be running. But as I look again, I see that, no, that's not true. It can't be. Where's Barton's partner, Sam? The two are inseparable. Or Marie's twin sister, Katie, the one in the wheelchair that Marie has cared for since their mother died? Marie wouldn't leave Katie alone in the house without anyone watching her. It's not a surprise that Timmy's mother isn't there—given the hour, she's probably three pints deep at Tricky Dick's—but why isn't he home doing his homework, or in bed? And why isn't Mr. Lindenbaum tucking his wife into bed at Greentree Nursing Home? It'll be lights-out there soon.

And where's Adelaide? I know she still lives in town, but I haven't seen her since she left. It's like she just vanished off the face of the Earth. One minute, she was an inextricable part of my life. The next minute she was just . . . gone. She hasn't called, or texted, or even accidentally wandered into the same aisle as me at the Foodmart. It's like she never existed at all. But she did. She was real. I know, because I can still feel her there, running beside me. She's not, though. The space she once occupied is empty. The space at my side. In my bed. In my life. Empty.

Most people running behind me are looking straight ahead, their expressions vacant, their pupils like the flat black circles from my Othello board game. A few of them, though, seem more alert. Their eyes are cast skyward, their chins lifted, their mouths twisted in expressions of abject horror. I turn my head and look up. What I see pushes a silent scream up my throat and past my lips.

The sky is on fire. A thin seam of flames stretches horizontally across the air, as if the night is a sheet of black paper smoldering at the top edge. My first thought is that I must be looking at the trail of a rocket or a missile streaking across the sky. But it can't be. The fire goes on forever, as far as my eyes can see, in both directions. It has no beginning and no end. It's infinite.

The fire is not what terrifies me the most, though. That's not what forces the scream from my lips. The real horror lies beyond the line of orange embers smoldering in the sky. It's as if I'm seeing past the torn edge of a tissue-thin façade, into another dimension beyond human comprehension. The depth of the darkness is unfathomable. It makes me think of black holes, of the deepest reaches of space, of what might have been there before the birth of the universe, before the sun, before the stars, before time itself. It is nothing. Naught. Zero.

It is death.

It's not the death of me, nor any person I know, nor death in any way that has been—or can be—understood by humankind. It's not death as described by religion or philosophy, by physicians or physicists, by the Bible or the *Necronomicon*. It's the death of reality, the disintegration of the fragile veil that humans' collective unconscious has draped over the true nature of the universe. It's the undoing of all that is done.

With a startling flash of insight, I realize I'm not being chased—I'm being *herded*. The thing behind me doesn't want to catch me. It wants to drive me forward into the void like cattle being corralled through the gates of an abattoir. *But why?* I wonder. And what is the thing, if it's even a thing at all? I can't see it, but I can sense its malign presence, a gravity-like force that propels me forward against my will. Even if I could stop running, I sense that I would still be pushed headlong into the abyss, like a corpse bulldozed into a mass grave.

A scream to my left tears me back to the present moment, and I turn my head just in time to see Elise Watson plummet through a hole in the street. No, not in the street. It's not a mere fissure in the asphalt; it's not a sinkhole. It's a fire-ringed rift in the reality of the street itself, as if the real world is a filmstrip stuck on a projector bulb until the celluloid melts. The hole reminds me of a solar eclipse, an irregular black circle rimmed with a blinding, brilliant corona that threatens to sear itself into my retinas if I look at it for too long.

Another breach in reality opens ahead of me to my right, swallowing the giant oak tree that has stood outside St. Mark's Church for generations. The hole widens rapidly, consuming the churchyard, then the steps where Adelaide and I posed for our wedding photos, then the church itself. I expect the steepled building to crumble into an avalanche of rubble as it falls, but it doesn't. Instead, it seems to fold in on itself like a papercraft art project stomped by an invisible foot. The sound is like a lit match tossed into a bucket of water: a quick, perfunctory hiss. Then, the building is gone.

More screams erupt as people behind me are swallowed by new fissures tearing through the fabric of reality. The flickering of the lights on Main Street intensifies until, somewhere above, a power line ruptures in a shower of sparks, followed by the blue-white flash of a transformer overloading. Every streetlight, storefront, and illuminated sign goes out at once, plunging the whole town into shadows.

With the darkness comes a new sound, a cacophony of sorrowful, spectral moans that rise and fall like a thousand whale songs droning at once. The wind accelerates to a punishing gale that blows directly into my face, stealing my breath as I try to inhale. My lungs fill with ash and soot; the smell of sulfur and ozone singes my nostrils and scorches my throat. My knees crack and pop and grind, bone on bone, cartilage seemingly worn away by the friction of the run. The skin on my face feels like it's sliding from my skull. Concerned, I touch my hand to my scalp, then draw it away in disgust. Giant clumps of my hair come with it.

The entire world is disintegrating around me. The seams of existence are fraying. Everything is breaking down. Everything is coming undone. Including me.

And then, I see her.

Adelaide.

She's walking down the sidewalk, her purse slung over her shoulder, oblivious to the chaos around her. She glances at her watch, then quickens her pace. She's late for something. An appointment? A meeting? A date? The wine bar where we met is just ahead—maybe she's going there? No, that doesn't make sense. She never drinks on a weeknight. And, besides, the world is ending. Can't she see that?

I try to call out to her, but the wail of the wind snatches the words away as soon as they leave my lips. She can't see me. She can't hear me. She doesn't even know that I'm here. I try to veer in her direction, but I have no control over my path. It's as if I'm on rails, locked into a specific trajectory, with no ability to course correct. I run past her just as she makes a left into the parking garage, the one where I kissed her next to her car after that night at the wine bar. I remember the flush of her cheeks, the warmth of her lips, the hint of Merlot still on her tongue. I cry out again, imploring her to turn around, to look at me. But she is gone.

Main Street is no more. A blazing line of fire bisects the road ahead, cutting directly through the center of Ace Hardware and across the street through Bill's Barber Shop. What remains is a precipice overlooking a vast chasm of infinite space and time, a living darkness seething with malevolence so immense that it dwarfs the gods of men. A darkness that hungers. That feeds. I should be afraid of it, but I'm not. I was wrong about being chased, about being herded. There's nothing behind me. I'm not running *from* something—I'm running *toward* something. Toward the darkness. Toward the edge. Toward the end.

And so I run faster, my legs pumping, my clothes aflame,

flesh peeling from my bones, until I am beyond the road, beyond the town, beyond Adelaide, beyond everything I've ever known, hurling headlong—smiling, screaming—into the void.

WARREN BENEDETTO writes dark fiction about horrible people, horrible places, and horrible things. He is an award-winning author who has published over 260 stories, appearing in publications such as *Dark Matter Magazine*, *Fantasy Magazine*, and *The Dread Machine*; on podcasts such as *The NoSleep Podcast*, *Tales to Terrify*, and *Chilling Tales For Dark Nights*; and in anthologies from Apex Magazine, Tenebrous Press, Scare Street, and many more. He also works in the video game industry, where he holds 50+ patents for various types of gaming technology. For more information, visit warrenbenedetto.com and follow @warrenbenedetto on Twitter and Instagram.

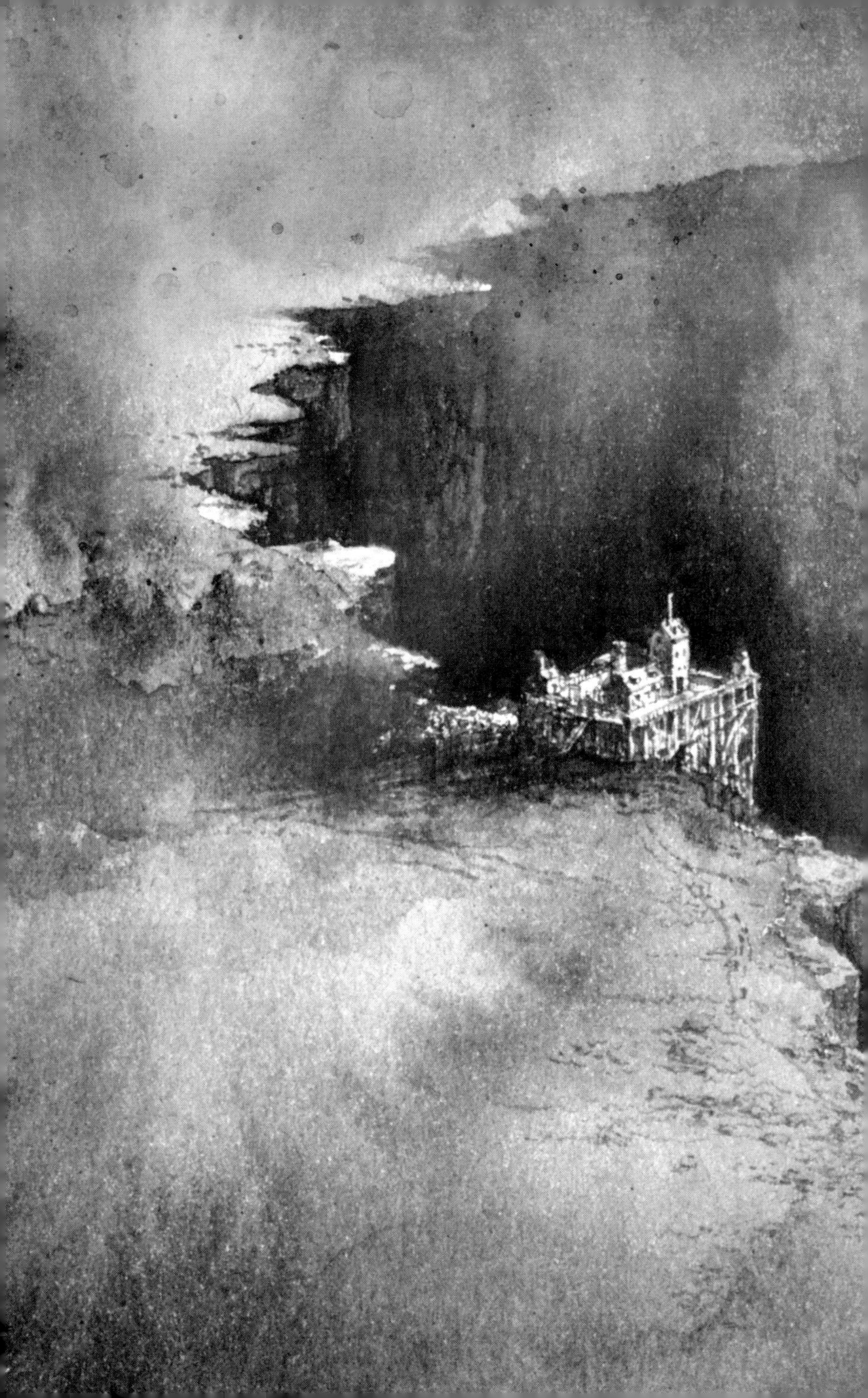

FURTHER READING

If you enjoyed this publication, be sure to check out the many other projects available under the Chthonic Matter imprint:

Nightscript
An 8-Volume Anthology

Twice-Told
A Collection of Doubles

Oculus Sinister
An Anthology of Ocular Horror

Come October
An Anthology of Autumnal Horror

Tenebrous Antiquities
An Anthology of Historical Horror

ABOUT THE EDITOR

C. M. Muller lives in St. Paul, Minnesota with his wife and two sons—and, of course, all those quaint and curious volumes of forgotten lore. He is related to the Norwegian writer Jonas Lie and draws much inspiration from that scrivener of old. His tales have appeared in *Shadows & Tall Trees*, *Dim Shores*, *Vastarien*, and a host of other venues. He has published two collections of his short fiction: *Hidden Folk* (2018) and *Secondary Roads* (2022).

www.chthonicmatter.wordpress.com

Made in United States
North Haven, CT
06 January 2025